Front cover artw
Amand

EXILED

From a Punjabi paradise to a
British building site

Jazz Bhangu

For my parents, without whose love, dedication, unrelenting support and unquestionable self-sacrifice I would have realised but a fraction of my potential. Thank-you for everything you have done for me.

CONTENTS

PREFACE

I am eternally grateful for the privilege of having witnessed and indeed intimately experienced a very wide spectrum of society. From a tough childhood in an inner-city, working-class, Punjabi immigrant family, to studying at Cambridge university, into the UK Armed Forces flying the Royal Family as a pilot, a stint in a high-flying corporate job in London and now living and working overseas as an airline pilot, in a company with employees from over one hundred and twenty nationalities. And throw in an enviable amount of travel, for both work and leisure; classic beach and adventure holidays - of course, but also frequent family trips to stay with extended family back in Punjab.

The more of the world and humanity I have seen, the more I have realised how fundamentally alike we all are. We all harbour the same cocktail of hopes, fears, aspirations, disappointments, insecurities. There are heroes and absolute villains, but for the most part, the world is full of honest folk, just trying to muddle their way through life's challenges.

But contrast this with the intensity of attempts from all quarters to polarise us. We are bombarded with campaigns to pitch black against white, one religion against an another, rich against poor. People are persuaded to sacrifice their lives fighting their brothers to defend arbitrary borders drawn by the very men whose primary objective was only ever to exploit them. Immigrants are vilified the world over. At least, until such time as they or their offspring make some revolutionary, commercially viable, innovative breakthrough, at which point they will be celebrated as a success of multiculturalism. We need look no further than Brexit or Trumpism to see isolationist zeal in full swing.

This book is my humble contribution to the struggle against factionalism. My small way of imparting a little of the most important lesson I have learned in my forty years on our amazing planet. And that is we need to stop looking for differences and instead take a moment to reflect and notice the commonality that is staring us in the face. Before judging and criticising others for their actions, really interrogate ourselves as to what we would do if we were thrust into their often highly unfortunate shoes.

The book is written as a collection of scenes that are presented in a non-chronological sequence. Some of these are clearly seminal for the characters, others less obviously so. But such is the way with human experience. Think through the defining moments from your own lifetime and you will likely compile a list that does not consist purely of events characterised by great accomplishments, celebrations or conversely acute sadness or loss. Graduations, weddings, deaths of loved ones will all be present but so will a multitude of other recollections that may seem trivial to others but are nevertheless etched deep into your mind. It is around those moments that this story is built.

The reader is also left to fill in the gaps between scenes, sometimes consisting of many months. This too is intentional. In life, there is no singular narrative that describes the absolute truth. We can all witness the same situation but perceive it completely differently, based on our own previous experiences and biases. Not only that, we will also then fill in any blanks in completely different ways, building a picture that is uniquely different for each of us but one with which we can personally closely relate. This is undeniably a human characteristic and something I wanted to foster, rather than provide a more detailed catalogue of events.

I hope you enjoy reading this book and joining the dots, in your own special way.

IMPORTANT NOTES

Foreign languages

U se of italics within quotation marks signifies conversation in a foreign language. Which language that is should be clear from the context.

Timeline

T o assist the reader, a graphical timeline at the start of each scene depicts where in the overall story that particular scene falls, chronologically.

SECTION 1: ENDLESS NIGHTMARES

'You gain strength, courage, and confidence by every experience in which you really stop to look fear in the face. You are able to say to yourself, "I lived through this horror. I can take the next thing that comes along".'
Eleanor Roosevelt.

1A. Amritsar, Punjab: January 2015

Year 2013 2014   2015   2016   2017

'**U**ncle a bastard terrorist, now this sister-fucking romeo wants to screw with Punjab Police? Want to go around creating bullshit drama and trouble *for no reason, do we? Mother-fucker!'* It wasn't the gob full of phlegmy spit splattering across his face that bothered Sukhjeet most. He hardly felt that, for his face was already numb and caked with a thick barrier of dried blood and perspiration. But the overpowering stench of the policeman's foul breath tore into his nostrils. Home-brewed liquor had blended potently with pungent lunch remains decaying in the multitude of crevices between his tormentor's stained, crooked teeth. Sukhjeet impulsively flinched, straining in vain against the thick hemp ropes attaching his tightly bound wrists to the rusty iron hook protruding from the ceiling of the interrogation cell. Baldev Singh about-turned like a newly recruited solider in drill training and then suddenly changed tack to stroll like a cat-walk model to the stout wooden stool at the far side of the cell, swinging his hips exaggeratedly from side to side as he went. He picked up the grimy, lime-scaled glass bottle positioned upon the stool, his tongue expectantly sweeping across his lips, preparing them for a final whopping swig. That would be the entire contents of the bottle polished off in one evening. Getting visibly more drunk as the 'interrogation' had progressed, Baldev Singh was acting increasingly unpredictably. Now, after giving his moustache a slow methodical twirl, staring into a non-existent mirror on the wall, he proceeded to stroll about the cell, shouting loudly, as if delivering an impassioned political sermon to an assembled crowd. It was when he was behind him that Sukhjeet found it most alarming. He laboured to shuffle around and look over his shoulders, ignoring the stabbing pain from his sore kidneys as he desperately contorted his body to keep the inspector in sight.

'*This time, I, Inspector, INSPECTOR, Baldev Singh,*

will NOT miss my chance to milk your parents for every-thing they have. EVERYTHING!' Suddenly, he turned and marched purposefully straight at Sukhjeet, whose eyes involuntarily shut themselves tight. It was a futile defence against the impending blows likely to rain down on his face again but nevertheless his only option. However, there was only a long ominous silence. Sukhjeet slowly opened his eyes, which was a struggle given all the swelling on his face. He discovered Baldev Singh's face only a few centimetres away.

'So, you ready to sign the confession yet,' he whispered, *'or do you need me to bring your pretty mother in and dance for us naked here before you agree?'*

Even to this day, Sukhjeet couldn't remember exactly what had happened next, it was so quick and impulsive. Baldev Singh stumbled backwards, dark blood starting to seep from the corner of his upper lip which had taken the brunt of the impact from his prisoner's forehead. Sukhjeet looked on helplessly, as realisation slowly dawned on the inebriated inspector and his grimaced expression quickly turned to one of intense rage. His face visibly reddened and began to contort. His eyes widened. Beady, black eyeballs surrounded by bloodshot whites stared directly at Sukhjeet like a starving, wild animal about to gorge on its prey.

'Mother-fucker!', shrieked Baldev Singh repeatedly, in a strangely high-pitched voice, as his face started scanning frantically left and right, searching unexplainedly around the cell. Sukhjeet strained to free his arms, but he knew his efforts were wasted. He instantly regretted what he had just done, though it hadn't been in any way a conscious move. An overwhelming, sickening fear started spreading throughout his body from the pit of

his stomach. His muscles involuntarily tensed, heartbeat rose and he found himself almost out of breath.

'I am sorry. Sorry. Please, please, let me go. I haven't done anything wrong'. Tears were starting to well in Sukhjeet's eyes. *'I beg you, let me go. I am like your little brother'.* But the words fell on deaf ears.

◆ ◆ ◆

1B. Wolverhampton, England: November 2015

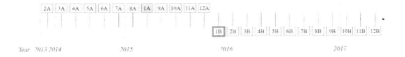

S ukhjeet jolted upright and knew immediately, from experience, that there was no chance of falling back asleep. The upsetting pattern of feelings he was now so familiar with made their appearance, exactly as they always did. There was short-lived relief that it was only a nightmare and he was actually not in that ghastly cell with Inspector Baldev Singh again. Followed quickly by utter despondency once it dawned on him that the original episode sadly had been real and that he was genuinely now here in this hell-hole of an existence, away from all his loved ones and everything he had ever cared about.

He mustered the energy to slide out from under the mass of thick, heavy duvets in order to exploit this rare opportunity to use the bathroom first, without having to queue and without risk of the limited hot water having run out. Careful to avoid awakening Raj in the adjoining bedroom, he slowly opened his curtains with small tugs, the grimy plastic hooks snagging annoyingly on the rail every few centimetres. His eventual view of the bright winter morning was obscured by an army of condensation droplets marching slowly down the panes of glass, starting to pool over unsightly, black patches of damp already present on the wooden window sill. However, he could still make out the unmistakable outline of a red Royal Mail van parked outside. The next-door neighbour was clearly running a little late for work today. You could normally set your clock by him leaving at 4.30am.

As he finished brushing his teeth, Sukhjeet glanced up at the small, round, heavily steamed-up mirror hanging crookedly off a nail above the sink, the plastic wreath around its edge unable to disguise its tackiness. Irrationally nervous about what he might uncover, he started mopping away the steam with the corner of his towel. As his face slowly appeared, looking intently straight back at him, Sukhjeet noticed just how much he appeared to have aged these past months. Thick, black stubble concealed most of the facial scarring but his cheeks had drained of their youthful chubbiness and rosy complexion. Dark bags hung under tired eyes and dry, flaky skin added at least a decade to his twenty-one years. Ironically, he had also tanned considerably since his arrival in the UK earlier that same year. An entire British summer toiling outdoors - twelve hours a day - mixing concrete or lugging bricks around, will do that to you. Affectionately known back home as 'Gora' ('white guy') by extended family, for his fair complexion and hazel eyes, his mother would endlessly regale how she had positively influenced such a supposedly outstanding outcome by proactively staying out of the sun and consuming inordinate amounts of creamy yoghurt during pregnancy. This happy memory broke a smile across Sukhjeet's face but was abruptly interrupted by Preetam's distinctively gruff voice and well-honed use of Punjabi vulgarity. *'Is that you in there Sukh? Make sure you piss into the actual bog rather than all around it like normal. I think your virgin cock is bent from excessive wanking. Come on, fucking hurry up too.'* Sukhjeet opened the door and walked straight past him. It was way too early for a conversation with Preetam. *'Good morning to you as well Sukhjeet brother... miserable fucker!'*

The roads were still quiet as Sukhjeet strode briskly to work. Thick frost covered parked cars and it was only his sturdy construction work boots that kept him from slipping on dense ice patches that littered the pavement. Feeling tiny ice crystals forming and then melting in his nostrils as he breathed in the freezing air, Sukhjeet lowered his head to bury his nose further into the woolly scarf he had reluctantly invested in only days prior.

It was the same route he took every day, six times a week. It took him past tall, red brick factories that, according to the blue plaques affixed to the walls, had been centres of engineering excellence in their heyday, producing aero engines, motorcycles and cars. It hardly seemed believable now. The doors and windows were all boarded up, covered with fresh graffiti overlaying multiple older, faded layers. Sukhjeet found much of it indecipherable; a blend of foreign languages, urban terminology doubtless only understood by teenagers, then splattered liberally with more common profanities.

Next, came the church, with its commanding spire and ornate brickwork. However, it was also in a sorry state of desperate disrepair. Grass and weeds had punched through the aging, tarmac car-park surface and the tall, blue parish noticeboard was literally being consumed by nature, rotten almost to the point of collapsing. A large concrete block, imprinted with '1860', was positioned above the high arched, wooden entrance door, revealing the age of the church. 1860; the height of the Empire and soon after the British annexation of the Sikh Kingdom in Punjab. Sukhjeet couldn't help but draw a direct connection between the plundering of his ancestral lands back home and the fact that at the same time even working-class neighbourhoods back in England were able to invest in such opulent places of worship. As he continued his walk, through the small park with its dated, wood-construction kids' adventure playground, the story of the Koh-i-Noor diamond making its way from the Sikh treasury in Lahore, to centrepiece of the Crown Jewels in London, played on his mind.

The first pedestrian he spotted on the streets that morning was an elderly Sikh woman, dressed in a dark, knee-length overcoat, with a scarf mostly covering her grey hair, hunched over sweeping the entrance of the local gurdwara – the Sikh place of worship. This was her chosen, personal act of servitude, humbly cleaning the steps in preparation for the daily trickle of devotees who would attend without fail, taking time out of their busy commutes to pay obeisance.

'Come in son, pay your respects to the Guru. And make

sure you eat something in the communal kitchen.'

'*Sorry bibi ji, I am running late for work.'* He wasn't, but it was all he could conjure up quickly.

'*The Guru gives you all the time you have on this planet. Try to take out a few minutes for Him every day too, son. Stay happy.'* She raised her hand and presented her open palm towards Sukhjeet as a blessing, before resuming her cleaning.

Sukhjeet bent down to touch the gurdwara steps and brought his fingers up to his forehead. It was out of respect for the old woman rather than the institution. But what was there to respect about her, really? Should he respect her fortitude and for the fact that despite all the kicking that fate inevitably would have given her throughout her life, she clearly had never lost her reverence for this greater being? Or should he pity her for wasting her time and energy in this futile cause? After all, what sort of God would generate so much suffering for His own entertainment? His thoughts drifted to his own parents, the kindest, most giving people he had ever known and steadfastly religious throughout their lives. Now look at them, their hard-earned wealth and ancestral property stolen from them, under continual risk of police harassment and unaware if their only son was dead or alive.

SECTION 2:
MORAL FIBRE

'You must honour your word and stand up for something, or else you are going to get run over by everything.' John Di Lemme.

2A. Amritsar, Punjab: November 2013

'**W**ow. *God must have sculpted you when he had a lot of spare time.'* Though only whispered, Satwant's intention was clearly for the passing trio of fresh-faced, first-termer college girls to overhear the flirtatious compliment. Particularly the tall, fair skinned one in the middle with the tightly fitting, pink and white, cotton kurta that showed off her impressive curves. Perched on his polished, maroon

Vespa moped, Armani shades propped low on his nose, meticulously neat, red turban, and sporting a pristinely maintained designer beard, Satwant usually managed to elicit at least a smile from even the most conservative of girls and this encounter was no different.

'*Hey, have you seen the pics of Mamta?*' asked Satwant, sliding off his Vespa and turning to face Sukhjeet in a sudden burst of enthusiasm, forgetting all about the girls, one of whom was still gazing fondly back at him.

'*Which photos?*' Sukhjeet sought clarification but should have guessed the answer.

'*Oh man, you have to see them. She has such amazing tits*' He paused momentarily, but failing to elicit any response from Sukhjeet, he opted to continue. '*Ouff...those rock-hard nipples. Apparently, Sanjeev fucked her and then said he would tell her parents if she didn't send him photos. I will WhatsApp them to you but don't forward around; don't want to completely ruin her life. Only for our enjoyment yeah.*'

Visibly agitated, his eyes closed and fingers massaging his temples to try and control the fury, Sukhjeet took the bait. '*How many times have I told you, do not send me this crap. Have some bloody decency man, she is somebody's sister.*' Sukhjeet opened his eyes to find Satwant now stood defensively with his arms crossed, inexplicably expressing surprise at the strong reaction his tale had provoked.

'*And how many times have I told you not to be such a goddam baba about it. She isn't YOUR sister, is she? So why do you care so much? Anyway, I am not the one who blackmailed her.*'

'*Fucking hell Satty, I care because it is so damn wrong.*' Sukhjeet put his hands on Satwant's shoulders. '*You have*

*a sister and tomorrow you might have daughters. Just re-
member, you reap what you sow.'*

'I haven't even done anything!' Satwant exclaimed.
'What should I do about it?'

*'You would go and smack Sanjeev in the face if you had
a shred of morality.'*

*'You go smack Sanjeev then, if you are such a hero,
bloody Bollywood superstar "Sunny Deol" over here'.*

And that is exactly what Sukhjeet did at lunchtime
that very day, in the bustling college canteen. Throngs of
students were queuing at the various food stalls, whilst
others wondered up and down the aisles clutching their
laden trays, searching for a vacant seat. Sukhjeet scanned
the room systematically, hunting for Sanjeev's conspicu-
ously shaven head and trademark studded, black leather
jacket. The 'Salads' queue was quickly eliminated; it consisted primarily of girls, giggling and gossiping loudly.
The 'Snacks' counter, as chaotic as ever, took a little
longer to inspect. Smoke billowed out from the kitchen
behind the counter and the noise of intense sizzling and
frying was audible even from the far side of the canteen. Orders were being shouted out before patrons even
reached the front of the queue, which the staff rightfully
ignored, instead more usefully yelling back details of orders that were actually ready for collection.

'Put me down for three samosas please.'

*'Ticket number three eight one. Chilly paneer one por-
tion and coke no ice.'*

'Three samosas please, I am in a rush.'

'Anyone, ticket three eight one?'

Just as Sukhjeet found himself getting distracted
with his enduring frustration over why Indians found the

concept of orderly queuing so difficult, he saw Sanjeev at the cash registers on the far side, near the 'Main Meals' counter.

There was no verbal exchange whatsoever and the incident was over in seconds. Sanjeev opted to stay put as a crumpled heap on the floor, covered in his lunch of steaming, hot rice and dhal, blood gushing from his smashed nose. He had fallen heavily from that singular right hook and having guessed the likely source of Sukhjeet's fury and experienced its intensity first-hand, he decided that cowering humiliated on the floor was his safest option. Feeling vulnerable, he tensed his body ready to absorb any further blows, whilst his brain desperately tried to work out what possible relationship between Sukhjeet and Mamta had sparked quite such violent retribution. However, much to his palpable relief, Sukhjeet turned around and calmly walked out the canteen. Sanjeev inhaled a deep breath as he saw Sukhjeet disappear through the double fire doors, predictably propped open with chairs in order to provide direct access to 'lover's lawn', where couples would often romantically dine alfresco during these temperate months, whispering sweet nothings and feeding each other morsel by morsel.

Within seconds, the pin-drop silence evaporated and the routine, chaotic din resumed. Most of the student onlookers in the canteen had heard about Sanjeev's role in the latest salacious scandal gripping the college and could therefore guess the root cause of the dispute. They quickly went back to their own business, apart from Anita Bains, a close friend of Mamta's. She remained standing still, expressionless, struggling to collect her thoughts that were now far away, somewhere outside the canteen, blindly chasing behind Sukhjeet.

◆ ◆ ◆

2B. Wolverhampton, England: January 2016

Sukhjeet had now worked his way up from 'hoddie', the term used to describe the building site brick-carrier. The lowest paid job, it had been back-breaking work. Running around for nine hours straight, trying to avoid vengeful, verbal abuse by ensuring that no bricklayer ever ran low on bricks. Endlessly up, down, up, down, flights of stairs, continually replenishing his empty hod with a dozen more bricks from fresh supplies stacked outside. He would reach home at the end of the day absolutely exhausted, routinely sodden through from his repeated exposure to the seemingly endless British rain. But his overwhelming memory was one of hunger. The bricklayers all took lunch breaks at different times, seemingly just to taunt him, so there was always somebody that needing topping up with bricks. Sukhjeet didn't even get the opportunity to sit down, rest his weary legs and eat whatever feeble attempt at lunch he had managed to prepare and bring along, though at best that would only be a couple of cold, rolled chapattis stuffed with the previous night's curry leftovers.

However, within a few months his wider abilities were noticed by supervisors. These highly sought-after practical skills had first been nurtured helping to repair the family tractor as a child. Sukhjeet had loved spending time in the barn with his father, a seemingly magical other-world, with so many tools and implements that could be improvised as toys. Initially, his involvement was limited to just watching his father's handiwork in silent awe. This progressed to occasionally being called upon to hand over a wrench or ratchet, or perhaps crawl under the jacked-up tractor or trailer and hold up a lamp. The culmination was his eventually single-handedly replacing an entire drive-shaft aged only sixteen. His mechanical engineering degree, or at least the two and a half years he managed to complete with flying colours before he was forced to leave India, meant he was now technically very capable albeit without the all-important certificate that proved this was the case. That one piece of paper, which meant the difference between his likely future reality of a lonely, borderline poverty existence versus a dream scenario of legitimate UK citizenship, a professional engineering job and the right to sponsor his parents to come join him.

These days his job was to install all the plumbing and gas fittings which would then get checked and signed-off by a certified technician at the end of the project. Working conditions had improved drastically but he had started to attract the envy of the other workers. The current team consisted primarily of Albanians and Bulgarians, who proved to be a difficult bunch to integrate with. They had always been cold towards him but since his promotion he found them entirely unwilling to co-operate. From pretending they hadn't heard him when he asked for help carrying heavy materials, to overtly refer-ring to him as 'paki' or 'nigger'.

'Sami, can you help me to carry these urinals up the stairs please?' asked Sukhjeet gingerly.

Sami's response was short and assertively deliv-ered. 'I am busy.'

'It will just take two minutes, please Sami.'

'Can't you fucking see I am too busy with MY job to do YOUR job as well?' Sukhjeet was about to walk away but Sami couldn't resist provoking him, supposedly speaking to himself, but in English and at a volume that suggested otherwise. 'This what happen when you hire some unqualified paki from some shit-hole country. His whole family living in mud-hut, pissing and shitting in street, but now he think he is plumber in England, able to fit bathroom.' He then said something, likely deroga-tory, in Albanian, before continuing in English. 'I have no idea why does British government let these people come here.'

The racket of plastering, banging, drills and paint-rollers on walls all suddenly ceased in unison and gave way to coordinated chuckles from every corner of the site.

'Nice one Sami,' came a voice from afar, followed by 'you're right' from the other side.

'Don't call me a "paki". To you, my name is Su-khjeet. And don't say anything about my country, you know nothing about me or where I come from.' Sukhjeet turned to directly face the tall Albanian bricklayer, who had no intention of diffusing the confrontation. Signifi-cantly older than Sukhjeet, Sami was definitely broader but no taller than him. He determinedly threw his trowel on the floor, making a loud clang, and stood up from his haunches. Dusting off his hands, he walked towards Sukhjeet, proudly thrusting his sizeable beer belly out in front of him. The two men squared up to each other, less than a foot apart. 'I call you what the fuck I want. We all call you what we want.' He took a moment to look around for affirmation from his colleagues, before continuing. 'What you do about it?' The intensity of Sami's clearly unjustifiable rage had put him in such a frenzy that he was starting to dribble tiny bubbles of spit from the edges of his lips.

It was a sudden but timely flashback that stopped Sukhjeet from acting rashly. He recalled an incident during his first days working in England where an encounter just like this, with a Pole that time, had led to a physical fight. The supervisor had witnessed the Pole's unforgiveable racist provocations yet still held Sukhjeet responsible, sacking him on the spot and forcing him to forfeit his wages for that week. Supposedly compensation to the company for plasterboard damaged in the scuffle and to the Pole for his black-eye, Sukhjeet knew that the simple fact of the matter was he could not risk involving the police due to his immigration status whereas the Pole had no such issues. So, he would always be the one exploited. As a result, he had learned not to rock the boat and somehow just got through each week; anything to get his hands on that pay-day envelope stuffed with three hundred and fifty pounds in cash. But something particularly bothered him today and he couldn't just let it lie.

Sukhjeet stepped even closer to Sami. There was absolute silence in the room and both men were able to hear each other's breathing. 'Sami, listen to me carefully. I am not Pakistani. I am a Sikh from India. My great-grandfather and grandfather fought for Britain in the World Wars so I have every right to be here, probably more so than you do. I don't want to argue with you. I will carry whatever I need up the stairs myself. But I am warning you for the final time, don't call me a paki again.' Sukhjeet started to walk away but turned back to deliver his last line, before Sami even had a chance to respond. 'And by the way Sami,' he said, taking a huge theatrical sniff of the air, 'use some fucking deodorant. Or, even better, learn to take a bath once in a while.' The audience erupted in laughter, louder and more boisterous than earlier, one of the Albanians even patting Sukhjeet on the back as he walked past. Smiling smugly to himself, he strolled off-site and to the local park to treat himself to a luxurious forty-five-minute lunch break.

Sat on a bench, he took a big bite of his filled chapatti and closed his eyes. Facing up directly towards the winter sun, he delighted in the warmth of the rays finding their way through his eyelids and flooding his mind with their soothing orange hue. He listened to the birds chirping in the trees. He took the time to relish the flavours in his mouth. And for those precious moments, all was well in the world.

SECTION 3: SUPPRESSED MEMORIES

'Happiness is short-lived, so enjoy every single moment while it lasts. And pain, just like happiness, comes with an expiration date. Learn as much from it as you can.' Chloe Hidalgo.

3A. Tarn Tarn, Punjab: April 2014

'S' *ukhi, son, hurry up. Come down and eat whilst it is hot'.*

'Coming mom. Just 2 minutes.' Though Sukhjeet knew full well that it would be way longer than that. He was having one of his dreaded bad hair days

and these were now critical moments ahead. The gel was drying fast, exacerbated by the ceiling fan that he had whizzing round at maximum speed in his futile attempt to avoid perspiring whilst getting dressed. But his side-parting simply refused to cooperate. Despite prolonged facial contortions and pouting in front of the full-length mirror on the door of his mahogany wardrobe, he remained unhappy with the overall look. There was nothing for it. He would have to re-wash his hair and start again.

Twenty minutes later, he walked into the dining room, hair styled and wet-look gelled to perfection, dressed in a flattering, plain, white Gap t-shirt and brand new, slim-fit Levi jeans. His mother was stood in the kitchen having finished cooking dinner, hunched over, methodically wiping flour remnants off the marble counter and collecting them in a cupped hand. She was dressed in a teal salwar kameez, black cardigan and wore an orange bandana to try and protect her freshly washed hair from the pungent odours of stewing masalas. Upon hearing Sukhjeet come into the lounge, she instinctively smiled before making an incredibly short-lived and totally unsuccessful attempt to appear annoyed.

'Ah…the prince graces us with his presence. Look what you have done. All the dishes have gone cold. Let me cook some fresh, hot chapatis for you.'

'No mum. I need to rush and I'm not so hungry - had a late lunch. Will quickly eat a few mouthfuls of this, it's fine.'

'Just like your father. I spend all day cooking and you both just scoff it down like cattle.'

'Here, have some fresh lassi, I just made it now.' She placed the steel cup of frothy milk on the table next to where he was stood, starting to eat.

'At least sit down to eat. Hai. What's so important you have to rush out at eight o'clock in the evening like a lunatic and...' She suddenly stopped mid-sentence and Sukhjeet felt his left ear being twisted sharply.

'Ouch! Mom...what are you doing?' he exclaimed, almost choking on a piece of pickled cauliflower he had just popped into his mouth. She was stood directly behind him so he was unable to inspect her face to confirm whether this unexpected brutality was playful or something more serious.

'Hmmm...now I understand.' She twisted a little harder for further dramatic effect. 'I have been wondering why the fair prince has been taking so long to get ready recently. Hair so perfect. New clothes. And now, he is covered in scent, smelling like a rose garden in spring.'

Sukhjeet could feel his face starting to blush. 'Mum. That really hurts,' he screamed agitatedly, his head now cocked at almost 90 degrees.

'Don't take me for an idiot Sukhi. I am your mother; I know you better than you know yourself.' She suddenly let go of his ear and moved around in front of him. 'So, who is she?'

'Who is who mum? I am in a rush. I have to go.' Despite his best efforts at keeping a lowered gaze and pretending to focus on finishing his meal, avoiding eye contact was proving difficult.

His mother's playful expression yielded to a more tender look. Her wide grin relaxed and her eyes glazed over a little as she fell into contemplation, deliberating on how best to broach this sensitive topic. 'OK Sukhi. You don't want to tell me who she is. But don't lie to me. Tell me this much. There is someone, isn't there?'

By now, Sukhjeet's mother face was close up to his

and they stood looking directly at each other. The multitude of shallow wrinkles spreading out across her face from her eyes did not detract from their magnificence. Unusually light grey in colour, with tiny streaks of green radiating out from her pupils, this extraordinary facial feature was the reason she was fondly referred to as 'Billo Massi' (*'Cat Aunty'*) in extended family circles. Undoubtedly, she was the primary source of his own strikingly good looks. After a few seconds of silence, she placed one palm on his cheek. *'Be a good son and tell me Sukhi. These are the things mothers live for since the day their sons are born.'*

Sukhjeet broke into a smile and lowered his gaze, partly embarrassed and partly overwhelmed by the unexpected emotional intensity of the situation. With a degree of tactility uncharacteristic even for her, she took the opportunity to kiss his forehead, having drawn her own conclusions. *'That's all the admission I needed Sukhi. But introduce me to my daughter-in-law soon; don't make your mother wait too long. Now go! Otherwise you will be really late.'* Then with one final playful twist of his cheek she released him.

It was a thirty-minute journey to Amritsar. Leaving behind the pot-holed dirt-tracks that fed into his village, Sukhjeet pulled on to the main road. With most families now congregated in their homes and settling down to eat dinner, the road would be largely deserted until he reached the outskirts of the city. Feeling invincible, chewing animatedly on a double dose of extra-strong breath freshening chewing gum, he opened up the throttle of his beloved Bullet motorcycle. The distinct thump of the powerful engine, the aggressive roar from the exhaust and the immediate acceleration were as intoxicating as the first day he had ridden this beautiful machine. He cut through the warm evening air, screaming past fields that were empty apart from the feint glow of lanterns in small brick huts situated next to irrigation tubewells, used by night watchmen to keep an eye on their employers' prized upcoming harvests. The occasional vegetable seller was spotted at the side of the road, either wheeling his cart home or making a last-ditch effort to sell any perishable goods at knockdown prices to bargain hungry commuters still on their way home.

The plethora of luxurious marriage parlours lining the sides of the road caught Sukhjeet's eye. He had ridden past these colossal, purpose-built wedding venues daily, for years, but today he found himself slowing down a little to peer more consciously through their tall gates, scanning the manicured lawns, impressively illuminated with arrays of overhanging coloured lights, leading up to lavish banqueting halls that could cater for thousands of guests. One day, he told himself. One day very soon.

His blissful fantasising was interrupted by a sudden barrage of discrete vibrations in his pocket. He brought his wrist up close to his face so he could inspect his watch, cruising along comfortably holding the handlebars steady with one hand. Shocked by the time, he immediately revved the bike back up to full throttle. He didn't need to pull out his phone to know that the messages would be from Anita. He was late for his date.

3B. Wolverhampton, England: May 2016

T hough work officially finished at 5.30pm, the wind-down would always start by 4.00pm on Fridays, thinly disguised as a formal tidy-up and mandatory tool inventory check. The upcoming weekend was forecast to be an 'absolute scorcher' and excitement filled the air at the building site. There was talk of drinking ice-cold lager to excess, barbeques, pub gardens, girls in mini-skirts and even one fancifully optimistic heralding of topless sunbathing in West Park. For Sukhjeet, weekends just meant wasted time during which he wasn't earning money. The current building site only operated five days a week so he had tried to look for alternative weekend work elsewhere and been successful on occasion but there was nothing reliable. Even the vegetable picking opportunities had dried up of late, contracted out to organised cartels of Eastern European or Chinese workers so no longer an option for a lone Punjabi.

The supervisor blew his whistle at 4.50pm and Sukhjeet was the first one off the site, squeezing through a gap in the towering, wooden hoardings. Most of the burlier workers couldn't manage this feat and were instead forced to walk all the way around to the main vehicular access gate on the far side of the site. Anyway, the others seemed in far less of a rush to depart. Instead, they stood around debating which pub they would frequent to 'wet their whistles', a term that had been utterly baffling for Sukhjeet until one of the newly arrived and extremely friendly Romanian plasterers explained it to him recently. However, one mystery remained. How could men who earned about the same as him, or even less in some cases. possibly justify spending three pounds on a pint of beer when they could buy a can from an off-licence for less than a third of that?

Sukhjeet walked home at a relaxed pace. The sun was slowly lowering on the horizon, its waning rays finding their way through gaps between buildings and trees to shine straight into his eyes, compelling him to squint almost continually. He opted to elongate the highly pleasant evening stroll by making a diversion into Phoenix Park, enticed in by the cherry trees in full blossom at the entrance gates. Inside, there were numerous football matches being played out, though the sheer number of goal boundaries marked out by blazers, rucksacks and water bottles meant it took Sukhjeet a while to work out which way the various 'pitches' were orientated and who was playing whom.

One particularly high-octane match caught his attention, especially the team defending the far goal. It included two players, both aged around ten, that showed real promise in Sukhjeet's opinion. The shorter, mop haired one just needed a bit more aggression in his tackling whereas the tall, gangly one could probably do with honing his ball control a little. Sukhjeet was daydreaming about how, given the opportunity, he would go about delivering his coaching tips to these promising stars of tomorrow, when the ball was kicked way out of play and landed only about fifteen metres away from the bench he was now sat on. Without a second thought, he jumped up and starting running towards it, barely avoiding tripping over himself after only his second step, having not taken account of his damaged knee's impact on his gait. By the time he composed himself and started towards the ball again, one of the kids had already covered the fifty-metre distance and retrieved it. It was a sobering realisation. From captain of the university first eleven football team and invariably the fastest sprinter on the pitch, to being outrun by a ten-year-old. He felt deeply bitter all of a sudden. The question that he purposefully kept deeply buried reared its unhelpful, ugly head again. Why him? Why him? No longer in the mood to watch football, he started walking along the path leading to the gate, violently kicking at a few blooming daffodils with his sound right leg as he went.

He soon reached the parade of shops on Dudley Road, consisting of: a combined Indian sweet shop and proudly egg-free bakery, a DVD rental store, an off-licence, a fish-and-chip shop and a post-office cum all-round general store. It was a busy time of day. Local workers, of both genders, of all colours, queued at the tills, eager to spend a little of their fresh weekly wages on whatever particular treat took their fancy. An elderly, Punjabi woman was hobbling out carrying a thin, blue plastic bag laden with five or six large, white bags of chips. A tall, young Jamaican man, with impressive dreadlocks, swaggered out of the off-licence with a pack of cigarettes in one hand and a litre carton of fruit juice in the other. The Indian sweet shop owner then appeared from the side-alley, wearing his knee-length, once bright white but now heavily stained cooking apron, sweating profusely. He was carrying an entire plastic crate of piping hot samosas, neatly covered in baking paper. He proceeded to load it carefully into a waiting customer's car boot; someone was clearly having a party tonight.

Just as Sukhjeet was reaching the end of this commercial stretch, he heard loud Punjabi music booming behind him. He turned to see a convertible, silver Mercedes, number plate 'RNB 74', coming to a screaming halt on the double yellow lines and a teenager jumping out the passenger door. Wearing a bright, red Liverpool FC football shirt, the boy looked around eighteen years old, as did the driver. Both had an identical haircut, almost shaven at the sides but heavily gelled and exceptionally tufted up on the top. Mr Liverpool FC disappeared into the off-licence whilst the driver started collecting rubbish from the back seat and simply dumping it into the road out the open passenger door, before reaching into the glove compartment for his sunglasses.

Unable to control himself, Sukhjeet paced urgently back towards the car, raging. 'Oi. What the bloody hell do you think you are doing?'

The driver was taken aback by the aggressive tone of the question. 'Chill bruv, you cool yeah. What's up man?'

The unnecessary illiteracy of the response only infuriated Sukhjeet further. 'I am not chilled. Why are you throwing all your rubbish on the floor like some sort of monkey? You are embarrassing our community.'

'You just pissed about that bruv?' He appeared greatly relieved and began looking gormlessly down at the McDonalds cartons and beer bottles, now lying at the roadside.

'And why the hell do you have the music turned so loud? Want to advertise to the whole town that you are a PUNJABI imbecile?'

At this moment, his friend emerged from the off-licence, clutching a four pack of 'Holsten Pils' beer, the warm, humid air already condensing into droplets down the side of the chilled cans. 'What's up Ranj? What's dis man's beef?'

'Nah, it's OK man. Bhaji is just chatting innit.'

'I am not "just chatting". I am telling your friend that if he is going to loudly advertise that he is supposedly Punjabi, he needs to make sure he doesn't make us look like a dirty community. Throwing his rubbish around the street like this. Disgusting.'

'OK. OK,' said Mr Liverpool FC, under his breath. He climbed into the passenger seat and once the car was safely starting to reverse back, he continued, this time loudly. 'I ain't takin' no shit from some jumped-up banana boat "bud-bud ding-ding" freshie yo. Go fuck yourself!' Having placed the beers in the footwell, he raised both hands to give a double V sign, keeping them elevated to maximise the offensive impact of the gesture.

Before Sukhjeet could react, the driver changed into forward gear and floored the accelerator, shouting 'whoa...fuck bro' with a gleefully excited expression plastered across his face, raising a hand to high-five his friend. Exhibiting an undeniably impressive acceleration, the car sped away. The last he saw of them was Mr Liverpool FC leaning down and elevating the music volume yet further.

Sukhjeet turned back around to continue his journey home, shaking his head in disappointment. As he turned the corner and walked along the wooden fence of the 'British Queen' pub's beer garden, he heard loud chitter-chatter and laughter emanating from the other side. He paused, momentarily considering going in, but quickly opted against such needless extravagance. Flavoursome wafts of charcoal smoke and grilling meat did find their way through but otherwise that fence was a seemingly impregnable barrier between two very different worlds.

SECTION 4:
GROWING UP

'Lust is to other passions what the nervous fluid is to life; it supports them all, lends strength to them all; ambition, cruelty, avarice, revenge are all founded on lust.' Marquis de Sade.

4A. Amritsar, Punjab: April 2014

'**Y**ou are late!' Anita was sat on the low wall encircling the ornate fountain in the middle of the impressively landscaped Ram Bagh garden, both feet dipping into the pleasantly cool water. Dragonflies darted about, seemingly without purpose, silent but for the ferocious beating of their wings. Anita had been observing them occasionally moistening their legs, dragging them lazily across the surface of the water, before landing for a brief respite on one of the many waterlilies bobbing around in the swells generated by the increasingly agitated splashing of Anita's feet as she had waited for Sukhjeet. She snappily turned her body forty-five degrees away from him as he finally approached, slightly out of breath from sprinting across the lawn.

'*I am sorry, dear love of my life. My mum held me up and then I had to wait for the security guard to clear off before jumping over the fence. We are not all as sexily slim as you that we can fit through the railings, darling, are we?*' There was no response. Even though the overt sweet-talking was not having an immediate impact, Sukhjeet was confident it would work over time. He tried to manoeuvre around to the side she was now facing. Anita turned abruptly in the opposite direction but not fast enough. Sukhjeet caught a fleeting glimpse of her smirk. Taking this as a tacit invitation to up the ante, he kicked off his shoes and jumped up onto the wall. He straddled her from behind, slipping his arms through hers and encircling her waist, his legs dangling either side of the wall. His one submerged foot quickly sought out both hers underwater, childishly prodding them a little, grateful they weren't flinchingly moved away and instead stayed put.

Anita was dressed in tight jeans, turned up a few folds at the bottom, exposing the feint anklet tattoo on her right foot. Her black t-shirt was so tight it almost seemed painted onto her, with a silver, sequined 'bebe' logo emblazoned across her chest. Keen to test the degree of acceptable intimacy, Sukhjeet leaned in towards Anita's neck, bare from her hair being raised up in a high pony tail, and started planting light butterfly kisses up and down her exposed skin. As he raised his head a few moments later and started nuzzling on her ear lobes, flicking his tongue over her discrete, gold ear studs, he couldn't help glance over at their reflection in the pool. Anita's feet had halted their earlier agitated splashing but the brisk evening breeze was still sending ripples shuddering through the water. Nevertheless, Sukhjeet could make out enough of Anita's facial expression. Her eyes were closed and her lips were slightly ajar, undoubtedly welcoming the attention she was receiving. Spurred on, Sukhjeet began to slide his hands up beneath her t-shirt. Anita reacted immediately to this, placing her own hands over his and pushing them back down gently. But the token resistance didn't last; she yielded within a few seconds, losing her struggle against the warm currents of euphoric excitement flowing through her every vein. His hands edged up her body, savouring her toned abdomen inch by inch. Unable to control herself, Anita let out a deep moan as she felt his fingers rub over her hard nipples, now projecting out unapologetically through the thin material of her bra.

'*Sukhi, please,*' she said in catches of breath. He wasn't entirely sure what she was trying to communicate, if anything at all, but he knew he didn't want to stop now. This was the furthest he had got with Anita, or with any girl for that matter, and he was on fire. He edged tighter against her so she could feel his hardness pressing against her back. She turned her face sideward and their lips locked immediately. It felt so right; this was just meant to be. Him and her, here at this time, under the stars, embracing, and tongues dancing passionately within fused mouths.

He forced his right hand up behind the cup of her bra, gorging on her pert flesh. His fingers determinedly caressed her stiff nipple and her reactions in response drove him wild. He could feel her entire body thrusting back towards him, her increasingly shorter gasps of breath, her hands stroking his hair frantically. She was all his.

Suddenly, she moved her mouth away and grabbed Sukhjeet's arm, more robustly this time, pushing it down away from her chest. Taking in a deep deliberate breath, she stared up into the night sky as she adjusted her bra and collected her thoughts sufficiently to express them, slowed down by the fog of passion still lingering in her brain. *'Sukhi, I love you. I really mean that. I have never felt like this about anyone before. I want to be with you forever. But I can't do this; not before we are married.'*

As he regained his own composure, his carnal desires subsiding slowly, the strength of his own emotions, in response to Anita's words, surprised him. Had Anita just proposed to him? He released his hand from her still-tight grip and brought it up to her face. Whilst tenderly stroking her cheek, he gently moved an errant lock of loosely curled hair back behind her ear. Anita had a very expressive face. Large saucer like eyes, beautifully naive and trusting, a sharp Punjabi nose and high cheekbones exhibiting a deep, pink hue from a combination of smudged blusher and blood still excitedly racing around her body. *'Anita, I, I mean….'* and with that he pulled her close and hugged her almost painfully tightly. *'I love you too, Anita.'* He was confused about why it seemed so much easier to say that without looking directly at her but he definitely meant it; he was absolutely sure of that much.

Only a few minutes later, they were out of the park and navigating the bustling, narrow lanes of the old city in

Amritsar, looking for somewhere to eat. This was prime-time for hawkers. The streets were crammed full of pedestrians shuffling along slowly, with the odd scooter causing mass annoyance but somehow ultimately managing to make steady progress through the crowds. All the hawkers incessantly pestered the crowds but one old lady particularly caught Sukhjeet's attention. Wearing a dark sari, with a huge red bindi adorning her forehead, she was only about five feet tall but was shouting louder than all her competition combined. Her inventory seemed to be entirely random, from colourful children's hand-held windmills, to padlocks, to a small supply of fresh runner beans! Sukhjeet's exploration into this bizarre collection of sale items was cut short by Anita suddenly stopping in the road and turning to face him. *'Oooh. I know. Let's go to "Kulvinder's Kulchas". I really fancy a radish paratha. Yum.'* Her excitement was unmistakeable. She even jumped a little and clapped her hands a few times. Even more than her widely admired good looks, it was this that he loved most about Anita. She had a contagious enthusiasm for even the most menial aspects of daily life, making her incredibly fun to spend time with.

'Whatever you want darling. Ready to give my life for you, so what is a paratha?' Sukhjeet delivered the response melodramatically and louder than was strictly necessary.

'Wow. I thought you studied engineering. However, now I think it must be a drama course you are enrolled on. But keep your voice down. No need to advertise your undying love quite so publicly.' Anita was giggling but her point was fair. Amritsar was a conservative city, not like the metropolises of Delhi and Mumbai where young adults could perhaps get away with frolicking in public.

They sauntered through a historic archway, its decrepit brickwork almost entirely covered with posters, some fresh and others peeling away, advertising everything from skin whitening creams, to new movie releases, to upcoming religious festivals. But the majority extolled virtues of prospective councillors, all equally untrustworthy looking, who would be standing for election in the upcoming voting. Electricity, telephone and satellite TV cables dangled low across the street. If you distractedly rode a motorcycle down here standing upright, these would take your head right off, Sukhjeet reflected, somewhat perturbed by this realisation.

'What thoughts are you lost in? Going to stand outside all night or are we going in?' Anita was standing with her hands on her hips, gesturing to the entrance of the restaurant with exaggerated movements of her face. Lost in his thoughts, Sukhjeet hadn't even realised that they had already arrived at Kulvinder's Kulchas, situated discreetly in one of the most confined arcades in the city. 'Age before beauty,' she mused, letting him enter first.

The first thing that hit them as they entered was the intense smell of the cooking. Mustard seeds popped in vats of oil giving off a bitter-sweet aroma, smoke billowed from ghee burning off of parathas cooking on giant hotplates and thick, sweet, milky tea simmered in a pot with cloves and cardamom pods darting frantically around the surface of the bubbling fluid.

Dinner was quick. That's the benefit of limited variety. In fact, there was no menu at all. Just choose the filling of your paratha and minutes later a thali would appear with your chosen centre-piece in the middle, piping hot, accompanied by sides of onion relish, pickles, butter and yoghurt. Anita had chosen radish and Sukhjeet opted for their most popular potato option.

There was a cacophony of noise in the restaurant: bhangra music blaring from the TV, children screaming, waiters shouting orders and clanging of thalis being collected from satisfied, belching diners. They themselves sat in relative silence for the first half of the meal, satiating their hunger with big mouthfuls of the delicious fare.

Anita pretended to be entirely absorbed by the food but was actually carefully observing Sukhjeet. He really was incredibly good looking. If it hadn't been for his shy, reserved nature, he would have had the pick of the college 'it girls'. Luckily for her, she reflected, despite his famed prowess as a footballer, he had traditionally been seen as quite nerdy and a bit of a 'mummy's boy' by most fellow students. That is, until the incident in the canteen with Sanjeev, of course. His beautiful, hazel eyes were summoning her towards him. She wanted to touch him but had to settle with nudging his foot under the table. To her slight annoyance, he ignored her tactility, seemingly genuinely pre-occupied with eating. Men! He had been infatuated with her an hour prior, she deliberated. But then he smiled. That incredible smile, accentuating his deep dimples and revealing a perfect set of teeth. Part of her suddenly wanted to be back in the park with him, playing out a different ending to that episode. But she would wait; it would be worth it in the end. And she would make sure they could be together forever, at any cost.

'*Which dreams are you lost in?*' inquired Sukhjeet?

'*Oh, nothing.*' Anita gave him a big smile back.

'*OK. Finished?*' Anita nodded, feeling satisfied and content in every way. '*Let's go then,*' suggested Sukhjeet, '*I will drop you back at the hostel...don't want you busting the curfew. But I don't have a spare helmet though so you will have to wear mine; I cannot risk anything happening to my sweetheart.'*

◆ ◆ ◆

4B. Wolverhampton, England: June 2016

Sukhjeet awoke, hot and covered in perspiration, summer sunshine beaming in through undrawn curtains. He glanced at the clock, bolting immediately upright when he saw '10:48', but then collapsing back into the damp sheets when he remembered it was Sunday. These sudden movements made him feel like he was being stabbed in the head and he took in a deep breath to combat the nausea. The sun was shining directly onto his face, further scorching his already discernibly parched skin. Frustration prevailing over his acute lethargy, he mustered up the energy to stumble over to the curtains and yank them closed, before flopping back onto his bed.

It was only now he realised that the bedside lamp

had been on all night and so he summoned the last remnants of his willpower to roll over and switch it off. As he did so, he felt a distinct sinking feeling deep in the pit of his stomach. Prompted by seeing an empty bottle of whiskey strewn on the floor next to his bed, memories from the previous night starting flashing before him. He desperately wished it had all been a dream but had to face up to what he had done. He raised the duvet to physically hide his face in shame, only lowering it again because he found it difficult to breathe the heavily musty air underneath.

The seed was sown by Preetam as they had sat in the garden, on upturned milk crates, drinking countless discounted cans of beer, enjoying the balmy evening. They had even treated themselves to lamb for dinner, expertly curried by Preetam, who had spent most of the day in the kitchen chopping, stirring, seasoning but also taste testing more than was surely strictly necessary.

'Just need to smash some pussy now,' said Preetam, in his typical, casually crude manner. *'Where do you go to get your end away, Sukh?'*

Sukhjeet avoided the questioning as long as he could before revealing that he had never visited a brothel in England, or in India for that matter.

Preetam's facial expression was one of genuine shock. His jaw physically dropped and he was uncharacteristically lost for words. Sukhjeet, himself surprised by the degree of Preetam's astonishment, wondered if there was something more to it and whether Preetam had in fact concluded he must be gay. But before he could clarify, Preetam found his voice again. *'You fucking serious brother? But you have been here over a year, right? Man, you*

41

are a saint. I would take you myself tonight but I only have sixty pounds left for the whole week. Had to send money back home for bloody high-school fees. They want next year's fees up-front already to guarantee a place for Bobby. Bloody thieves. Doesn't matter though, it is the best school in the area. Hopefully he will get educated and not have to work for these mother-fucking, racist white men in a foreign land like his dad.'

'White men didn't ask us to come here, Preetam. We came because of our own personal difficulties, whatever they might be. We earn our daily bread here. We shouldn't speak ill of the very country that feeds us and even gives you the opportunity to educate your kids and build a better future for them back home.'

He raised his can of beer towards Preetam who, always game for a toast, mirrored the gesture enthusiastically and responded with, *'you really are a saint Sukh. Bring the house down!'* With that, Preetam gulped down the remaining half of his can in one go.

Preetam returned purposefully from the fridge with the last two cans, having now regained his trail of thought. He opened both and handed one to Sukhjeet. 'Cheers'. Preetam took a gulp, leant forward and started whispering, albeit unnecessarily, as nobody else was home. *'Seriously bro, I will tell you exactly where to go.'*

'Preetam, I am not visiting a hooker.'

Preetam tutted. *'Oh ho. Just hear me out. She is one hundred percent hot and clean. Pakistani Punjabi. These Muslim women really know how to treat their men. Don't know her real name but customers call her Chhamia. She is clean too and only fifty pounds a shot. 101 Burns Road – just opposite the liquor shop. I am getting a hard-on just thinking about her.'* Preetam stood up and stretched both his arms out horizontally in front of him, before thrusting his hips rapidly back and forth, mimicking sex with an imaginary Chhamia, tantalisingly positioned ready for him on all fours.

Sukhjeet couldn't help but burst into laughter and they high-fived each other before Preetam supposedly called it a night, though Sukhjeet suspected the dirty bugger would actually be awake in his room a little while longer yet!

As he sat alone, watching the sun finally setting, his thoughts wandered to Anita and how much he missed her. Her laughter, her passion for everything in life, her incredible smile. And, spurred on by the half crate of beer inside him, his thoughts moved quickly on to recollections of her firm body. He finished his remaining beer and went inside, locking the back-door behind him. The thought of going to sleep already was depressing so he convinced himself he would head out to buy a bottle of whiskey, though that neither explained why he took seventy pounds in cash with him nor why his heart was pumping so hard in his chest during the short walk to the store.

For almost an hour he sat in the small park, next to the off-licence and newsagents store, opposite 101 Burns Road. Alone, he pondered and drank, mixing large measures of whiskey with coke in the plastic tumbler that was reluctantly provided free of charge by the sour faced Indian lady behind the till in the off-licence. From here on, his memory started to get hazy but there was still enough to piece together the remainder of the night. The front door of number 101 being opened by a large woman, dressed in traditional Punjabi attire. Wandering into the hallway, with its heavy-duty, plastic carpet protector and woodchip papered walls. Looking across into the living room, filled with smoke, its dark orange, paisley pattern carpet, where a number of bald, overweight men were sat playing cards.

Being asked in English by the woman, 'Romanian, Bengali, Pakistani…what you want?'

Replying with simply one-word, raising the pitch at the end to make it seem like a question. 'Chhamia?'

Handing over fifty pounds. Walking up the stairs, as directed. Past the three rooms on the first floor, all of which had their doors closed but couldn't withhold the noise of the ongoing business inside. Up another set of stairs, into the loft room.

He found Chhamia sat on the bed, staring blankly towards the door. The first thing that had struck Sukhjeet about her was the wildly bedraggled hair. She wore a bright green, knee-length kameez but the salwar – the bottoms to the outfit – were strewn on the floor. Her eyes were droopy with dark circles hanging below, contrasting strongly with her otherwise fair complexion. The image haunted him and he sensed that all too familiar sick feeling strengthening inside as he continued to recollect events.

She had gestured to Sukhjeet to close the door and, as soon as he did, she removed her kameez and lay down with her legs wide open.

She was entirely shaven so even from a few metres away Sukhjeet could see raw redness and swelling around her crotch. He also distinctly recalled her dark nipples and the way her breasts sagged to either side of her as she lay down, withered beyond their years. Even at the time, he had wondered how many men had cruelly yanked and pulled at those over the past months or even years. Poor girl. He remembered how despite not feeling any attraction to this woman whatsoever, he was hard in seconds, just seeing her lying there naked. For self-imposed expediency, he had only taken his trousers and boxers off, leaving his t-shirt on. To his relief, he did distinctly recall walking over and putting on a condom, taken from the bowl-full that had been lying on the bedside table. He had no idea if he had done it properly though, and she had definitely seemed beyond caring whether he even wore one or not.

He had finished in seconds. Afterwards, Chhamia had continued to lie on the bed, completely motionless, as she had been throughout the brief act. He recollected discarding the condom, getting dressed and walking out with his half empty bottle. His last glance at Chhamia had revealed her starting to rise sluggishly from the bed and reach for the tissue box. He hadn't even made it to the end of Burns Road before throwing up the first time. He had then stumbled back home, swigging straight from the whiskey bottle as he went, throwing up a further two times during the journey, gently sobbing to himself all the way like a madman.

SECTION 5: AGONISING SOLITUDE

'Call it a clan, call it a network, call it a tribe, call it a family. Whatever you call it, whoever you are, you need one.' Jane Howard.

5A. Patiala, Punjab: May 2014

'**W**ow *Gora!*' said Taya Ji, referring to Sukhjeet tenderly by his childhood nickname. '*You grew up to be even taller than me. Looks like my sister-in-law has brought you up eating fresh butter and drinking full cream milk, eh? Good to see. Come and give Taya Ji a hug.*'

Sukhjeet had a real soft spot for his dad's elder brother. He had moved to Odisha, eastern India, a decade prior when Sukhjeet was about ten years old, so they only saw each other at big family occasions now. But during Sukhjeet's early years, when they had all lived under one roof, Taya Ji, as he was respectfully known, would always be spoiling Sukhjeet with gifts of exotic, imported chocolates, colourful, cutting-edge kites, prized Real Madrid football shirts and once even a pair of genuine Nike trainers. To this day, Taya Ji had no kids of his own so all his love and affection had been *'destined by God for Sukhi'* as he always used to say. Though still a real character, sporting a bright orange turban, flowing, largely white beard and perfect handlebar moustache, he had aged considerably compared to how Sukhjeet remembered him.

Sukhjeet moved on to greeting his aunt in the traditional manner. *'Sat Sri Akal Tayi Ji.'*

'Have a long life, son,' she replied, touching her hand on his head, which he had already lowered in preparation to receive the blessing.

'You will need to bend down more than that. Your Tayi Ji is only four foot tall remember.' And with that quip from Taya Ji, the entire group broke into laughter. Just like the good old days, when they used to sit huddled together on charpoys in the courtyard of their ancestral home, eating dinner, drinking sweet hot milk, regaling stories of the adults' childhood days and cracking jokes for hours on end.

They had all assembled at Sukhjeet's aunt's house. His father's only sister, the eldest of four siblings, was hosting the entire extended family for her only son's wedding. Poohah Ji, as she was known, had lived in her marital home in Patiala, many hours' drive from Tarn Tarn, since before his birth, so Sukhjeet had only met her a handful of times. They were now very well-to-do. The family she had married into was like his own, traditionally middle-income 'Jatts' – farmers. But the huge upsurge in rural land value, fuelled by flourishing demand for housing developments in Punjab, had meant that the sale of only a few acres had propelled them into a level of prosperity they were not accustomed to. This 'new money' was evident everywhere Sukhjeet looked. From the huge but undeniably gaudy, brand new villa built in time for the wedding, the SUVs parked in the drive, to the extravagant wedding decorations and illuminations covering the entire compound. Throngs of migrant workers from poorer Indian states zig-zagged between the guests serving cold drinks and snacks. Clearly uncomfortable in their starched white shirts and bow-ties, most didn't even speak Hindi, never mind Punjabi.

'Can you English speaking? I said double whiskey. This is rum.' In desperation, the man grabbed another guest who happened to be stood close to him. '*My friend, explain to this guy. I have no idea what language he speaks.*' Before the confused man, whomever he was, could explain that he obviously didn't speak Bhojpuri either, the Punjabi head contractor appeared, clearly flustered from the abuse he was receiving from all quarters.

'*Oi mister. What kind of joke is this? Why have you hired waiters that don't understand a word of what we are asking for.*'

'*I am sorry sir ji. Please tell me, what would you like.*'

The man decided to switch from Punjabi to English in order to add weight to his complaint. 'But this is not the point young man. You will wonder around to each guest yourself only to get their orders? Then what will this army of waiters be doing. They have come to enjoy and dance in the wedding only or what?' However, he quickly realised that the longer this interaction lasted, the longer it would be before he got his drink. His solution was to order an entire tray of whiskeys and a few glasses of ice, so that he would not need to bother with the waiters for a while.

The wedding was still a few days away but tonight was 'mayiaan' night – a combination of important pre-wedding ceremonies. By the time evening approached, Sukhjeet and his family were comfortably settled into their rooms, had changed into their evening attire and made their way into the courtyard at the rear, where a huge marquee had been erected. Sukhjeet's father wore a freshly tailored, white kurta pyjama with waistcoat, his maroon turban and matching pocket square coordinated perfectly with the colour of Sukhjeet's mother's salwar kameez. Sukhjeet opted for a more casual look; grey trousers with a long, black, traditional kurta top, white embroidered stitching lining the hems, cuffs and collars. He had deodorised heavily, anticipating a sweaty evening.

At the centre of the cavernous marquee, the groom, Sukhjeet's cousin Bikram, was sat on a wooden footrest, dressed in an old t-shirt and shorts. In front of him lay an impressively artistic formation on the concrete floor. Created by Bikram's younger sister, Jaya, rice dyed in numerous bright colours had been arranged to construct an intricate and beautiful matrix on the floor. A perfect square was created using white rice as a border and then partitioned into eight identical wedges using yellow rice. Each wedge then filled with differently coloured rice, the result was truly a fitting epicentre to the ensuing ceremony. The 'batna' ritual was ready to get going. Bikram's mother and aunts heralded the official start by proudly holding up the corners of a large, square, heavily embroidered red and gold cloth, creating a majestic canopy over the groom. They then burst into painfully discordant recitals of traditional folk songs, wishing him a fertile wife and fruitful marriage. Throughout the singing, groups of well-wishers would come and rub a pre-prepared mixture of turmeric, flour and milk into the poor boy's bare arms and legs. Supposedly to ensure that his skin 'glowed' on the big day, uncles, aunts, cousins, even neighbours took their turn. The male cousins, as always, waited until last, so they could introduce a little mischief. Whereas everyone else settled with rubbing a little of the sticky, yellow goo on Bikram's forearms or shins, the boys went straight for entire fistfuls into his beard, hair and even down his shorts, much to everyone's bemusement. Once everyone had their turn, the ceremony was concluded. Bikram disappeared to have a shower and everyone else settled into their seats for the evening's festivities.

Large vats of freshly cooking delights simmered on industrial scale stoves set up in the make-shift kitchen just outside the back of the marquee, from where fragrant trays of food were being hurriedly ferried in and distributed liberally. There were plates of spicy, red chicken legs and masala lamb chops for the men-folk who were sat drinking liquor on the tables closest to the bar area. Meanwhile, the women were busy gorging on the multi-coloured sweets of all varieties proudly on display near the front.

Soon enough, fuelled by excessive sugar and invigorated yet further by copious helpings of strong, sweet cardamom tea, the women broke out into traditional 'giddha', a no holds barred affair where even the most demure and shy would engage fully in edgy poetry recitals alongside bouts of wild and often suggestive dance moves. The menfolk quickened their drinking, not feeling anywhere near intoxicated enough to face the inevitable dragging onto the dancefloor by wives, sister-in-laws and aunts; no-one felt safe.

As the evening progressed, the liquor began to kick-in and dance floor dominance shifted gradually from the women to the men. 'Giddha' was replaced by a local DJ starting to play upbeat bhangra. Energetic dance-offs between the male cousins became the order of the day. It was time for the women to raise the tempo and make their come back, but this time the men were up for it. Out came the 'jago' - a sizable, traditional, hollow, steel kitchen vessel, ornately dressed for the occasion in rich, red, embroidered velvet, with half a dozen lit oil candles affixed to the top. As the DJ sped up the beat, the 'jago' was passed systematically amongst the family members, who would place it on their heads and then assume centre-stage on the dance-floor. Recorded for posterity by multiple cameraman, everyone took the opportunity to exploit their moment of fame, proudly exhibiting how much they could thrust and gyrate whilst still balancing the contraption on their head, without using their hands.

Not wanting to be outdone, the more inebriated menfolk brought out the 'chajh'. Historically used for sieving grain, it was an A3-sized, mesh tray made of tightly intertwined and bound straw. Using a thick wooden bar, the men took turns to strike at the tray, goading each other to hit harder. Eventually, one of the distant uncles put down the whiskey bottle he was inexplicably, but not uncommonly, balancing on his head, forcibly took hold of the 'chajh' and smashed it to smithereens with the bar, the crowd cheering and applauding in unison. Within seconds, the waiting staff appeared from the shadows to clear away the debris of straw remnants now littering the dancefloor. Shortly after, Sukhjeet saw his father and Taya Ji, both of whom were teetotallers, subtly lead the man out the tent for a breath of fresh air.

Sukhjeet was having an absolutely great time. He loved these get togethers. Sounds of joy filled the air, expressions of happiness greeted him everywhere he looked, elders bestowed their precious blessings on him at every turn. Why couldn't life always be like this? Perhaps it could and indeed perhaps it would. After a vigorous round of bhangra, even raising Bikram on his shoulders at one point, which was no mean feat, Sukhjeet returned to his chair for some respite. He sat alone, glugging chilled lychee juice and mopping his drenched brow with a napkin. His kurta top clung to his back and he made a half-hearted attempt to unstick it and allow it to dry a little but truth be told he was having too much fun to be fretting about the state of his clothes. As he caught his breath, observing the dancefloor in full swing, he started day-dreaming about how much more fun these events would be in the near future with Anita by his side. He imagined her, dressed in a bright Punjabi 'lengha' dress, him in a fancy suit, the star new couple, impressing all the onlookers with their coordinated dance moves.

Turning down a drink from a yet another uncle, and now bored of explaining that he was teetotal like his father, he opted to return to the dancefloor for the final hour of dancing that remained.

❖ ❖ ❖

5B. Wolverhampton, England: July 2016

S ukhjeet walked back from work as quickly as he could. Ominously dark clouds hung precariously in the increasingly gloomy sky and a brisk breeze had picked up, quickly dispelling the familiar scent of earthy humidity that had lingered all day. He zipped up his jacket as high as he could but the wind seemed to tear right through the thin fabric itself. This was his second British summer but the variability of the climate was still a major source of bewilderment. He was beginning to understand the rationale behind the national obsession with weather and concluded that he too probably needed to start paying more attention to forecasts on the radio. Though only 5.30pm, the dreariness made it feel a lot later. Streetlights were automatically starting to illuminate and living rooms along the entire road were lit up.

Sukhjeet cursed as a gurgle from his stomach suddenly reminded him that he had nothing at home to eat. Purchasing groceries would entail a detour to the Aldi supermarket, significantly increasing the probability of his getting caught in the almighty storm that was clearly brewing. He opted for the fish-and-chip shop as a solution. Such extravagance was normally limited to weekends only and even then, only once. The only logical solution was that, as pay-back, he would have to abstain this coming weekend, cooking dhal at home instead.

He stood alone in the shop, waiting for the fresh batch of chips to finish frying. Triggered by the smell of batter, familiar noise of loudly bubbling oil and occasional swirling of the vat's contents with a large, steel strainer ladle by the shop attendant, he started daydreaming; a flashback to his childhood.

On his way back from primary school, he would be able to smell pakoras cooking even before he got to his wide-open courtyard. But there was still the excitement of finding out what flavour they would be that particular day; spinach, paneer, cauliflower. He would run into the kitchen, sometimes actually yelling with excitement, only to be told by his mother to first go and change out of his school uniform.

'Why can't we have pakoras everyday mom? And why do you make some flavours some days and different flavours other days? How do you choose which flavour? And why are we only allowed one small plate?'

'Why don't YOU stop asking so many questions and just eat Sukhi, son!' his mother would say, giving his nose a little twist or kissing him on the forehead as she placed the plate in front of him. 'Only one plate though. Fried food *is bad for you. If you eat fried food, all the other meals that day should be extra healthy to make up for it.'*

'Two pounds forty-five please, pet.' The attendant waited for a few seconds before prompting Sukhjeet again. 'Yow am OK, anything else?'

'Oh, sorry.' Sukhjeet moved his hand away from his cheek, where it was subconsciously stroking his scar, and handed over the exact change he had ready. 'Also, do you have any salad ma'am?' The portly attendant, probably in her early thirties, winced, thinking he had just called her 'mum'.

'We have coleslaw. Eighty pence a tub.'

'What is...err...col-sla...' Sukhjeet's voice trailed off as he realised that he had no idea how to pronounce that word. He had barely caught it with the attendant's thick Black Country accent.

'It's like a salad. Yeah. Cabbage, carrots and mayo and all. Yow will like it, goes a treat with chips.'

Sukhjeet understood something about carrots and cabbage so was surprised to be handed a tub full of something white, out of the fridge.

'Tara-a-bit, pet.' The attendant handed Sukhjeet his change and returned to a bar-stool to continue intently watching a wildlife show about crocodiles on TV, using the remote control to put the volume back to the unnecessarily high level it had been at when Sukhjeet had first walked in.

As Sukhjeet emerged from the shop, the sky had darkened further and he thought he could feel isolated specks of rain landing on his face, though there was no sign of them on the pavement yet. He slung his rucksack off his back and popped the purchases in. This would have to be a speedy walk back home.

Despite his urgency, he couldn't help but glance into houses on the way, as he walked past. In almost all, he could see schoolchildren, of all ages, in their uniforms. Some were slouching on the sofa watching TV, some grazing on crisps or bumper packs of sweets and others playing video games. Many were glued to their phones, no doubt messaging their friends even though they had spent all day with them. The smell of cooking dinners filled the streets. Indian aromas were present for sure but there were also plenty of other alien fragrances all mingling in the clammy air. Dogs up and down the street barked and howled, almost in chorus, excited by their respective owners returning home from work or school and hopeful for some tender, loving care and even more importantly, food.

He was making good progress and was now only about six or seven minutes away from home. Taking his standard route, he turned off the main road and into a side-street, where he saw the indicator lights of a parked, family saloon flashing a few times, as its central locking was remotely activated. He looked across the road to see a middle-aged man with a briefcase, dressed in a nicely fitted, dark suit, pop a set of car keys into his pocket just as was greeted with a discreet kiss from his wife at his front door, which was opened for him even before he reached it. She was wearing a cooking apron and had her hair in a mass of pink, plastic curlers. Sukhjeet slowed his pace momentarily and subtly craned his neck to peer into the nicely carpeted hallway. Two adorable toddlers raced towards the man, dressed only in their nappies, clutching at each of their father's legs when they reached him. The man slammed the door shut by kicking it backwards with his foot but through the frosted glass Sukhjeet could make out two pale, little bodies being elevated high into the air.

Sukhjeet felt a wave of despondency wash over him. He knew his feelings towards this man, whom he knew nothing about, were entirely irrational but he couldn't brush them off. Sukhjeet was convinced that the man had no idea how fortunate he was. He probably thought he had a really difficult life, not enough money, career progression difficulties and God knows what other irrelevant problems he made up in his mind. But in reality, it seemed clear to Sukhjeet, that this stranger's situation was probably as enviably close to realistic perfection as it came. To not appreciate such privileged kismet every moment of every day was unforgiveable.

As these irrefutably toxic thoughts percolated in Sukhjeet's mind, his pace instinctively slowed yet further for the remainder of the journey. The rain really started to pick up and by the time he reached home, he was completely soaked. Yet still, he strolled unhurriedly up the garden path, which was just a wobbly line of paving slabs thrown onto the overgrowing lawn. Thick curtains were drawn across all the windows and the house seemed to be entirely empty. He turned the key and pushed open the door, hearing the familiar sound of yet another weekly delivery of junk mail being shoved aside. The pervasive, musty odour seemed stronger than normal, as he made his way down the dingy hallway into the kitchen.

Having discarded the mouldy tea bag sat disintegrating at the bottom of the only mug he could find, Sukhjeet half-heartedly rinsed it out before filling it up with tap water. He sat quietly, feeling even more alone in the world than normal. His having to occasionally steady the wobbly, wooden table turned out to be an unexpectedly welcome distraction from his dark thoughts. Consumption of his special fish and chips treat satiated his now diminished hunger but the meal provided no real enjoyment. He kept the kitchen light off throughout and blankly stared out the window into the gloomy garden, watching lightning illuminate the overcast sky, the silence of his solitude punctuated by the associated, explosive bursts of thunder. It was only when he had finished and started clearing away the packaging, that he realised he hadn't taken any notice of what the coleslaw had even tasted of and whether he liked it, though he had eaten the entire contents of the tub. He scraped some remnants onto his index finger and licked it clean. Nothing could be further from what he had wanted when he asked for salad.

SECTION 6:
HEARTFELT
PRAYERS

'The magic of our first love is the ignorance that
it can never end.' Benjamin Disraeli.

6A. Amritsar, Punjab: May 2014

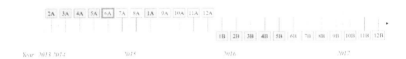

Anita texted Sukhjeet to say she was running late and to wait for her at the *'Flour Market'* entrance to the Sri Harmandir Sahib complex. Known locally as Darbar Sahib and globally famed as The Golden Temple, this was the ever-bustling holiest of holy Sikh shrines.

The visit to Darbar Sahib was entirely Anita's idea, conjured up whilst lying next to Sukhjeet on a secluded patch of parched lawn near the college sports pitches one afternoon the previous week, with overhanging branches of a peepal tree shading them from the intense heat. They had been trying to decide how they should fittingly spend their upcoming 'last day' together. The pressure was on to think of something noteworthy as an unwelcome reality had recently dawned on them both. They almost certainly would not see each other until the university re-opened in September, after the painfully long summer break, unless Sukhjeet could magically conjure up a way to visit Anita in Delhi. However, he had no relatives there so accommodation would be problematic, as would finding a convincing excuse to give to his parents as to where he would mysteriously be disappearing to for a few days.

Sukhjeet again repeated his preferred option for the day. Anita to try and persuade her room-mate to stay with another friend that night and for Sukhjeet to finally stage the much-debated, illicit attempt to gain entry to the girl's dormitories. *'You are crazy Sukhjeet. You heard about the guy who got caught doing that the year before we enrolled? Principal Madam expelled him permanently,'* Anita exclaimed. *'I also heard that his parents kicked him out of their house after that...and that he committed suicide because he couldn't cope with life on the streets.'*

'Seriously, Anita, that story gets more and more embellished every time I hear it. It started off as only a two-week suspension from university when Satty first told me told me about it a few years back and now look where it has reached... poor boy is dead! Anyway, that aside, I cannot understand why Principal Madam is so against boys and girls mixing. Just because that cow is on a mission to die a virgin, she wants us all to suffer the same fate. Damned witch.'

'*Sukhi! Don't say that,*' Anita was desperately trying to hold back her laughter as she twisted her body to reach over and punch him on the arm.

'*What? It's so true. She would frighten off any suitor. She has more hair on her monobrow than her entire head. Ever seen a normal woman with a short boy's haircut like that? And she wears huge size ten trainers with a sari. Proper weirdo!*' Anita was in fully fledged fits of giggles by then and had to prop herself up on one elbow so she could breathe.

Wiping away tears of laughter from her eyes with the back of her hand, Anita attempted to refocus the discussion on the pressing matter at hand. '*Sukhi, there will be plenty of time for all that when we are finally together...F-O-R-E-V-E-R.*' She made a kissing motion with her lips before her face adopted a sombre expression and her gaze drifted into the distance. Sukhjeet glanced over in the direction she was staring and saw nothing of interest. Just a few gardeners in green overalls, who were lethargically pruning the hedgerow that bordered the pitches. Just as abruptly, Anita looked back towards Sukhjeet and articulated her concerns, in an uncharacteristically downbeat tone. '*Sukhjeet, I don't want any distance to come between us during these months apart. I couldn't bear to lose you.*' Anita shook her head from side to side as she spoke, a subconscious, physical manifestation of the apprehension she was feeling. Sukhjeet had still been working out how to react to the sudden change of mood when Anita continued, with a resolve in her voice that made it clear whatever she was about to say was not up for debate. '*I know what to do on our last day. Let's go to Darbar Sahib together and ask for God's blessings to keep our relationship safe.*' This surprised Sukhjeet as he previously had no idea

Anita was even remotely religiously minded. However, the revelation was certainly well received. His own family were devout Sikhs though he had always been free to adhere as much or as little as he wanted. Most visibly, his parents hadn't kept his hair unshorn as a child. *'He can grow his own hair long if he chooses to as an adult,'* his mother had always said. That wasn't a choice he had made yet. Though, whenever he visited a gurdwara, he did wear a turban. And there was no doubt about his inner convictions. He was a strong believer in God and liked to think he lived up to the core values of his faith as he understood them: absolute equality of man and woman; a strong revulsion against caste-based divisions in society; and, a genuine desire to stand up bravely and defend those that he saw were being wronged.

So, as instructed, Sukhjeet waited patiently for Anita near the arched gateway at the top of the steps leading up from the *'Flour Market'* entrance, having removed his shoes and washed his feet at the dedicated area for this at the bottom. Despite the soaring summer temperatures, a natural breeze tunnelling through the narrow passageway made it just about bearable, though he was starting to perspire nevertheless. Perching himself on a marble step, he made the most of this rare opportunity to really examine and appreciate the exceptionally ornate structure around him. Normally, he only attended on religious occasions and getting through the entrance was a wrestling match with the throngs of devotees converging from all corners of Punjab and indeed India, cramming their way through to gain access to the main internal quadrangle and pay their respects at the shrine itself.

The entrance was still in its original brick and stonework, with elaborate and impressively detailed, hand-crafted designs carved into covings and pillars. However, multiple bullet marks disfigured these beautiful historic walls; poignant reminders of the battle that was fought here between Sikh militants and Indian Army forces in 1984. It was difficult to imagine scenes of such violence and bloodshed playing out in this abode of absolute serenity and calm. As Sukhjeet sat sombrely contemplating the fate of so many slayed, innocent men, women and children who were caught up in the carnage, he completely missed Anita walking up the steps. She tapped him on the shoulder and he was greeted by her beaming smile when he turned to look up at her. Totally losing his trail of thought and jumping immediately to his feet, he barely resisted the temptation to give her a hug, which would have been entirely inappropriate, of course. She looked angelic, dressed in an elegant but simple, cream coloured Punjabi suit and a dupatta covering her head. Her make-up was very light, but served to further accentuate her naturally warm facial features. Sukhjeet was lost for words; he had only ever seen her in Western clothes before.

As was often the case, Anita was left to break the silence, 'Wow...Mr Singh, looking VERY smart today.' She smiled and gave him the universal OK sign with her thumb and index finger, taking in how he looked with a turban, which is how he would be adorned on their wedding day. She decided the look really suited him and made a mental note to discuss with him later whether he might want to become a 'sardar' one day – a turban wearing Sikh. They started walking, in silence, their feet negotiating the staircase down the other side into the main compound in perfect step, both with their hands reverentially held together in front of them. As they entered, the din of the city disappeared behind them, replaced with soothing sounds of harmonium and melodious recitation of divine verses, emanating from within the shrine, the centrepiece of the complex. The gold leaf covering this eminent structure glistened, reflecting the intense rays of sunshine back out in all directions as if it were the original source of the illumination. No matter how many times Sukhjeet visited, he was always awestruck upon first viewing this vista. The beautiful, golden structure in the centre of this expansive, deep-blue, perfectly square reservoir was truly a sight to behold.

Standing distracted in utter awe, it took a few seconds for it to dawn on them that the wide marble floor bordering the reservoir was searing hot. But sensing the heat melting their bare soles soon enough, they hopped undignifiedly but in unison over onto the straw carpet that had been rolled out for that exact reason. Following the marble walkway around, they eventually joined the queue leading to the Darbar Sahib itself - the revered, golden shrine and centrepiece of the complex. Sukhjeet popped on his sunglasses to shield against the glare from all the bright, white marble, as they patiently waited in the queue on the singular walkway leading from the edge of the reservoir to the shrine in the middle. Thankfully, an awning was erected along the entire length of the walkway, providing some respite from their exposure to the unrelenting heavenly rays.

To their mutual relief, they only had to wait about fifteen minutes before they reached the front of the queue. Glancing at each other briefly, they stepped humbly through the doorway together. This was one of four identical entrances facing out in all directions, a physical manifestation of the core Sikh tenet that anyone from any corner of the Earth was always welcome. The resident *'reader'* was sat perched behind an elevated copy of the Sikh holy text, the Guru Granth Sahib, quietly reading from it. His impressively long beard swayed in the breeze created by the manual wafting of a Chaur – a ceremonial instrument consisting of a silver handle from which sprout long yak hairs. This was continuously, reverentially fanned through the air, to keep flies and dust away from Guru Granth Sahib. Adjacent to this central arrangement sat the three musicians, two playing harmonium and one animatedly tapping away on a tabla, all beautifully singing memorised holy verses at the same time as playing their instruments. They were dressed identically in white kurta pyjamas, pristinely tied orange turbans crowning their heads and matching orange, cotton scarves draped around their shoulders. Despite all that was going on, rather than any sensory overload, Sukhjeet and Anita both felt the deepest possible sense of peace and tranquillity. When their turn came, they knelt, bowed to Guru Granth Sahib in unison and, as pre-planned, both asked their Creator to protect what they valued most in their life - their love.

6B. Wolverhampton, England: September 2016

S ukhjeet was relieved to see he wasn't the only member of his college class running late that evening. They acknowledged each other with the briefest nod of their heads and slight mumble of 'hello' before Zainab and Sukhjeet ended up walking uneasily up the college stairs and through the corridor, alongside each other. Sukhjeet positioned himself slightly behind her, awkwardly accelerating past every few minutes whenever there was a door for him to hold open. Slightly embarrassed by the sheer number of times this chivalry had to be repeated before they reached the classroom, Zainab kept her head lowered and walked as fast as possible, adeptly adjusting her bold, blue patterned headscarf as she went, smoothening it out around her shoulders and neck where the wind had ruffled it.

'Ah, Zainab and Sukhjeet. Come in. I thought maybe the forecast of heavy tonight rain had put you off.' Mr Humphries was a man evidently struggling to cope with the modern world. Nobody really knew what to make of him, with his insistence on the continued use of outdated overhead projectors and acetate slides, his love for tweed suits and eccentrically unkempt, curly, ginger hair and sideburns.

'Sorry, sir' said Sukhjeet, instantly realising how stupid that sounded and quickly taking his place at a lone, empty seat on the second row, trying not to attract any further attention.

Sukhjeet's command of English was superior to any of the other students. He was here for one reason only. His mother had always yearned to see him in graduation attire. That seemingly assured reality had been cruelly snatched away from him only months before it had come to pass. But if he had to start from scratch in Britain to realise his mother's dream somehow, then he vowed to do it. Right now, this adult education English language college course was the only option available to him, so here he was.

The lesson actually turned out to be interesting enough. It transpired that although Sukhjeet's grasp of English grammar was very good, it had been mastered by rote learning in his village primary school classroom and through never-ending examples completed as homework during his high-school years. For the first time in his life, he was now formally being taught the underlying rules and principles that governed the language. However, the sheer complexity of the various conventions and vast number of exceptions to every rule made it seem way less logical than he had previously thought it to be. The magic of this incredibly influential language diminished in his estimation.

'Don't worry Sukhjeet, even us native speakers struggle with it,' said Mr Humphries, noticing the slightly perplexed look on Sukhjeet's face during a discussion on plural forms. He paced around the room as he recited; "If I speak of a foot and you show me two feet, and I give you a book would the plural be beek? If one is a tooth and a whole set are teeth, why shouldn't two booths be called beeth? If the singular's this and the plural is these, should the plural of kiss be ever called keese?' It was at this point that Sukhjeet caught Zainab's eye. They both smiled uneasily and then urgently and symmetrically lowered their gazes to the floor to look intently at nothing in particular. The next few moments were a haze and before Sukhjeet knew it everyone around him was starting to stand up and pack away their books.

As Sukhjeet started making his way out of the classroom, he realised that Zainab was only a few feet behind him, so, impulsively, he held the door open for her, ensuring to keep his eyes lowered. It was only after about thirty seconds of still being able to see her feet stationary from the corner of his eye that he looked up to find her stood facing him with her hand outstretched.

'We haven't actually introduced ourselves to each other. My name is Zainab.'

Sukhjeet was taken aback. 'Oh, yes, err my name is Sukhjeet Singh..err...as in...Sukhjeet. How do you do ma'am?' he said, omitting to even shake her hand in his excited bewilderment.

Zainab tried to withhold her laughter, now withdrawing her own arm and instead bringing her hand up to her mouth in a clenched fist, forcing her fingers firmly against her lips. Her face was tightly scrunched together in a vain attempt to stay composed, making her large, green eyes, lined with kohl and adorned with long, fluttering eyelashes, yet even more prominent. Her nails were painted a deep red and Sukhjeet couldn't help but note the lack of any rings on her fingers. Suddenly, unable to control herself anymore, she burst out into torrents of laughter, completely doubling over as she did so. Not entirely sure what was quite so funny, Sukhjeet did regardless find the outbreak highly contagious and quickly both were in synchronised giggling fits, Zainab having to hold onto Sukhjeet's forearm to steady herself.

'I am so sorry. I suddenly felt like I was in a black and white movie or something. No one has ever called me "ma'am" before. I didn't mean to laugh, so rude of me.' The apology was made less sincere by the fact that she was still wiping tears from her eyes.

'I just got a bit surprised when I saw you standing there. Don't worry, you made me laugh too. I haven't laughed this much in a long time.'

They slowly edged their way out the classroom and started to head down the corridor. As they peered out the hallway windows into the unwelcoming, cold, dark night, it was clear to them both that a torrential downpour was underway.

'Listen, it is raining really badly outside. Want to grab a coffee and wait until it calms down a bit?' Zainab seemed entirely relaxed, contrasting sharply with Sukhjeet's obvious nerves. He was also somewhat pre-occupied with determining the source of her accent. He was no expert but there was a strong, mysteriously seductive, European twang to Zainab's well-spoken English.

'Coffee? Us? Where? I mean, there is no coffee shop near here?' Sukhjeet asked quizzically.

'There is the Costa machine near the computer room. Let's grab a hot drink and we can chill on the comfy seats. Come on.'

Zainab was already starting to lead the way. As she walked ahead, Sukhjeet caught a sweet, jasmine aroma of perfume lingering in the air, enticing him to follow closely. Her overcoat was slung over one arm whilst she held her handbag in the other, a bright yellow umbrella poking out the corner. He found himself a little spellbound, transfixed on her hips swinging from side to side, beige trousers contouring her shapely legs very closely, leaving little to the imagination. They flared out suddenly near her feet, with a six-inch slit revealing the bottom part of her stylish, brown leather boots. He felt totally out of his depth in this situation and could feel his heart palpitating.

Sukhjeet insisted on paying for the coffees, thankful that he had sufficient change in coins for the dispensing machine. He was already planning to recover as much of this expense as possible by, weather dependent, attempting to walk home rather than catching the bus. For himself, Sukhjeet selected almost exactly the same as Zainab had ordered – latte with one sugar, but just not 'skinny' in his case. Milk with its creaminess and fatty nutrition extracted was the biggest con ever as far as Punjabis were concerned and Sukhjeet shared this sentiment entirely. As he walked back slowly, carefully balancing the precariously overfilled polystyrene cups that were brimming with froth, he noticed that Zainab had sat down on one side of a double sofa. Without any conscious thought, he automatically gravitated towards the empty double sofa opposite and gingerly sat down in the middle.

'Thank-you,' said Zainab, lifting the cup to her mouth with both hands, in a single, smooth manoeuvre that also incorporated a 'cheers' gesture towards Sukhjeet. She took a gulp, closing her eyes as she did so. 'Oooh. That's better.' Light brown foam covered her upper lip, blending seamlessly with her bronze lipstick.

The conversation flowed easily, primarily because Zainab seemed happy to take the lead, describing her life in significant detail. She was Palestinian but had been living in the UK for ten months now, working in New Cross Hospital, Wolverhampton, after her initial six months in Birmingham. She had immigrated from France where she studied for three years to become a nurse. She spoke fluently in Arabic and French and her spoken English was reasonable. However, she wanted to improve her command of English grammar and technical writing skills as she felt this weakness would be a barrier to advancing up the nursing ranks. Sukhjeet was hoping to avoid talking about how he ended up in the UK by keeping the conversation focused on Zainab, firing out a continuous barrage of questions about her life.

'Do you have any other family in UK then?' he queried.

'That's an easy one. None at all. I have an elder brother in France, working for a family friend in their textile business in Lyons. That's the closest family.' Eventually, the briefest of pauses in their conversation opened the gates to the feared but inevitable reciprocal questioning. 'So, what about you? Tell me about your life. Do you have anyone here?' Zainab took a large gulp of her coffee and leant back, ready to listen attentively to Sukhjeet's tale.

'No, I don't have any family here.' The abruptness of the response created an awkward silence which was once again left to Zainab to eventually break, which she did, returning her torso back upright from the reclined position she had only just adopted.

'Look, it's fine. You don't have to talk about your background if you don't want. Let's talk about something different. She started pointing towards Sukhjeet's left leg. 'Hey, I noticed you were limping a little as you climbed the steps earlier. What have you done? Let me guess, football injury? You look like an athlete of some sort for sure.' Zainab was smiling playfully which put Sukhjeet a little less on edge whilst he worked out how he would respond.

'Actually, it's an old injury, from before I moved to UK.'

'Ouch. Accident?'

'Yes, sort of an accident.'

'Must have been a bad "sort of an accident" to still not have healed. You should get it looked at by a professional. Do you know any doctors or nurses?' Zainab laughed and Sukhjeet felt himself starting to blush a little.

She continued with what was objectively an entirely reasonable conversation thread but to Sukhjeet was already starting to feel like an interview. 'What about the scar on your cheek?' Unnecessarily, he thought, she then raised her hand and started stroking her own right cheek to further stress the point. 'Is it from the same accident?'

He looked up, now directly at Zainab, making clear eye contact for the first time. She was strikingly beautiful by any measure. Her headscarf and the virtuousness it signified only added to her allure, though Sukhjeet was definitely having trouble reconciling Zainab's undoubtedly bold, outgoing personality with a headscarf. Back home, an Islamic headscarf would most likely have pointed to a degree of conservatism that he just didn't see in Zainab. But it wasn't lost on him that all these stereotypes were based on his very limited interactions with young, modern Muslim women, having grown up in a part of India largely devoid of this community. Extreme violence and bloodshed during the painfully sad partition of India, in 1947, of which Amritsar was an unfortunate epicentre, had caused them to flee to the newly formed Muslim state of Pakistan, as reciprocally uprooted Sikhs and Hindus migrated east to India, as refugees in their own country.

However, he wasn't distracted by these anthropological reflections for long and found himself promptly resuming his unabashed admiration of her attractiveness. Her most striking feature were those emerald green eyes, the most remarkable he had ever seen. They utterly captivated him and he had to consciously pull his gaze away, actively fighting his inner compulsion to continue staring. She actually didn't seem to mind. In fact, if anything, she found herself savouring the attention and was happy to wait patiently for his answer to her question. Except Sukhjeet was lost for words. It had just dawned on him that since he arrived in England over a year ago, Zainab was the first person to ask him about his ailments. She was the first one who had cared.

SECTION 7:
HUMANITY'S WOES

'A patriot must be ready to defend his country against its government.' Edward Abbey.

7A. Tarn Tarn, Punjab: Jun 2014

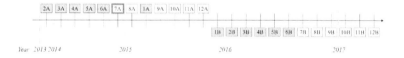

'**S** *at Sri Akal Uncle Ji.*' Sukhjeet politely greeted Vir Singh, one of his father's longest standing friends. The duo had known each other since high school days and Sukhjeet's father often regaled tales of their mischievous adolescent antics, be it; deflating the schoolmaster's bicycle tyres, stealing mangoes from neighbouring fields or bunking school to attend a local funfair. However, judging from the glint in his father's eyes when he recounted these memories, Sukhjeet strongly suspected that the really juicy stories were being withheld. Now retired from a government service job, Vir Singh still lived in his ancestral home a few villages away but would often stop by when running an errand into town, continuing to rely on his ancient but trusted, lime-green Bajaj scooter for transportation.

'*Sat Sri Akal Sukhjeet. Come, sit with us.*' The two men were the same age but Sukhjeet noticed how Vir Singh's longer, whiter, wispier beard made him look so much older than his father. He accepted the invitation, collapsing into the comfortable, white leather sofa opposite the two men. The intense heat was incredibly fatiguing so sitting in the only air-conditioned room in the house was an inviting prospect. '*Grab a cup and pour out some tea. Your mother has filled up this pot way too much. Our old bladders cannot take it these days.*' The ensuing impish chuckling was short-lived, halting suddenly when Sukhjeet's mother popped her head around the door to see if anyone wanted anything else. It was as if the two men were teleported back in time. Like they were suddenly juveniles once again, sat at the back of a classroom misbehaving and the teacher had unexpectedly spun away from the blackboard to face and admonish them.

Once Sukhjeet's mother took her leave, Vir Singh turned back to Sukhjeet's father. '*So, what were we saying? Ah yes, so, you see, right now, everyone is talking about the thirtieth anniversary of the massacre at Amritsar. The next generation is singing songs about it and raising slogans about human rights, retribution and demanding answers. But those of us who lived through those dark days, we just want peace. There is not a single household in these villages that wasn't impacted. My nephew for example, whose story you know well. My sister still thinks he might walk through the door one day. He disappeared twenty-five years ago. Your younger brother, Joginder, God bless him. He was such a good Sikh boy. At least you were able to carry out his last rites but what a state the police left him in.'* He took a deep breath, closed his eyes and meditated on God's name for a few seconds, repeatedly whispering *'Vaheguru'* quietly, shaking his lowered head as he did so.

'Vir Singh Ji, I agree with you. There is nothing to be gained by agitating people on this issue. Only bloodshed lies down that path. However, the truth needs to be uncovered. Otherwise what's to stop history repeating itself?'

'Daddy Ji, what actually happened with Joginder Chacha Ji? queried Sukhjeet. He knew his Chacha – his father's younger brother - had passed away a few years before Sukhjeet was born and he knew it had been under traumatic circumstances, somehow involving the police, but he had never gotten the full story.

Vir Singh answered on behalf of Sukhjeet's father, *'son, let's leave this subject. Talk about something...'*

'No Vir Singh Ji, I disagree with you on this point,' interrupted Sukhjeet's father, cutting Vir Singh off mid-sentence. *'He needs to know. We cannot hide the facts from him forever. It was a blood relation - his real Chacha, yet the poor boy has absolutely no idea what happened to him. I always protected Sukhjeet from this part of our family history because it's too horrific for a child. But take a look at him now.'* His father half raised a hand in Sukhjeet's general direction before continuing, *'he is a fully-grown man. This is the right time to tell him. We owe that much to the next generation.'* Vir Singh remained silent but looked uncomfortable, clearly unconvinced. Sukhjeet's father continued, looking up towards the ceiling as he began to recount the sorrowful tale, reliving the details in his mind's eye. Sukhjeet found himself leaning forward on

the sofa, intent on not missing any details.

'*Joginder was studying at Khalsa College, Amritsar. This was around 1989, five years after the viscous Indian Army attack on Darbar Sahib in 1984. You will no doubt know all about that – "Operation Blue Star" – a deliberate strike at Sikh sentiments under the rouse of flushing out terrorists and arms. And then, of course, there was the government orchestrated, genocidal slaughter, looting and rape of thousands of innocent Sikhs in Delhi some months later, following Prime Minister Indira Gandhi's assassination by her Sikh bodyguards.*'

'Yes father. It's never been covered in school but I have seen the bullet marks at Darbar Sahib and also read a little about that period on the internet.'

'Yes, these days youngsters can get any information from this internet. Not like in our days,' Vir Singh muttered to himself, head lowered.

Sukhjeet's father continued, stroking his beard as he spoke. '*Well, following those harrowing events, a Movement became established to liberate Punjab from India, to create an independent Sikh homeland, Khalistan. This was a grass roots movement, supported, at least in the early days, by most rural Sikh families. We were all sick and tired of how Sikhs were being treated by the central government of India, to shore up majority Hindu votes across the country.*' Sukhjeet hung onto every word. He had only ever overheard his father talk politics with other men but this conversation was directed at him. For the first time, he felt he had a place at the adults' table. '*Joginder was actually not really into all this. He kept himself to himself. However, there was a big event at a gurdwara near his college where the police allege fundraising for armed Sikh outfits took place. The police arrested a few innocent local boys and gave them the "special* treatment" in prison, asking for names of organisers of the event. After a few hours, they ended up giving names of anyone they could think of, just to escape the pain. One of the names was Joginder's.' His father leaned forward to pick up his teacup, blew the milk skin aside and took a loud slurping gulp. *'Joginder had certainly been at the event but was just doing his routine, voluntary service at the gurdwara that day, serving food to the visitors, helping in the kitchen cleaning utensils, the usual. Well, a few days later he was arrested in college, man-handled out of a classroom and taken to the police station. The principal of the school immediately drove to see your grandfather at home and raise the alarm. So, within a few hours, your grandfather gathered the village elders and some local officials he knew and arrived at the police station, demanding Joginder's release. I think they paid quite a lot of money to the Inspector but I am not sure of the exact details. Anyway, they managed to get him released. He had been badly bruised up. He wasn't in possession of his turban anymore and tufts of beard had been pulled out too.'*

'Vaheguru, Vaheguru,' Vir Singh repeated under his breath, head still lowered.

'Well, Joginder changed after that,' said Sukhjeet's father, resuming the tale after a few seconds of contemplation. *'I think he knew that no matter what he did now, it was only a matter of time before he was picked up again and again. It was the standard way the police extorted money from families with a bit of land, like ours. Around the same time, Joginder heard a story related to a good friend of his, Ranjit. I can't remember his surname. He was from the next-but-one village just here. He had gone "underground" and joined the Movement some months prior. Anyway, the police had arrested his sister to apply pressure to him to hand himself over. She was released after a week but committed suicide a few days later, unable to live with the shame of what had happened to her inside police custody.'*

'*Vaheguru, Vaheguru,*' Vir Singh continued to utter, his eyes remaining closed throughout.

'*So, Joginder also went underground. I remember the day he went.'* Sukhjeet could see his father's eyes welling up. '*The whole family went to the gurdwara to pray. Your grandfather told Joginder never to be fearful and to always reflect on the great Sikh martyrs and their sacrifices whilst fighting tyranny.'* He paused whilst he leaned forward to grab a corner of his kurta to wipe away his tears. Vir Singh handed him his own handkerchief. '*Your grandfather told him not to worry about the family and that we would remain in Chardi-Kala - high spirits. Of course, I could tell it hurt my father deeply but he was a very resolute man. I have told you how he was in the British Army and how bravely he is reputed to have fought against the Japanese in the jungles of Burma. There is that story where his section of only six Sikh soldiers was ambushed by a Japanese platoon of thirty men. He managed to climb up a steep hill, under continuous enemy gunfire, single-handedly kill four Japanese soldiers and then take control of their machine gun, forcing the others to call off their attack and flee. To this day, his medals are framed and displayed on Taya Ji's living room wall, in Odisha.'* He paused to smile, proudly recollecting the story, which Sukhjeet had heard before but was happy to listen to again. '*He was tough, strong in mind and with an indestructible spirit. But it really broke my mother. Joginder had been the baby of the family and my mother had really spoilt him with treats his whole life. She was already not well but passed away a few months after Joginder left. Probably for the best, at least she didn't live to see what we went through after that. You see, once the police found out about your Joginder Chacha leaving,* they would visit our house incessantly, to harass the family and try and get one of us to disclose Joginder's whereabouts. They arrested your Taya Ji once too. Your grandfather managed to get him released after paying a lot of money to a very corrupt police constable from a nearby village who brokered a deal, the notorious Baldev Singh. That dog is an Inspector now, a SHO - Station House Officer. Unbelievable. Anyway, after that, your Taya Ji was sent to Odisha for his own safety. Your grandfather sold some land to settle the loans he took from friends to pay the extortion money and also to allow your Taya Ji to set himself up over there.' Sukhjeet's father took a break to compose himself and Vir Singh filled the void.

'During those days, your father started sleeping over at mine most nights. The biggest fear was that the police would now arrest HIM one night after darkness fell, for that's when they would come to apprehend innocent young Sikhs and generally hound families whose sons had joined the Movement. Fortunately, by this time, your father's sister, your Poohah Ji, was already married and living safely away from here with her in-laws in Patiala.'

Sukhjeet's father continued, clearly intent on telling the full story. 'Things got really bad then. There was a huge crackdown across Punjab and the police implemented a no questions asked "shoot-to-kill" policy. Kill anyone that even looked like a sympathiser. Long beards, orange turbans, kill them. It was a truly nightmarish time. And then, one night, there was the noise of a jeep pulling up outside our courtyard walls. It beeped its horn loudly a few times and then drove off. But your grandfather ignored it. In those days, you never opened the door at night. Either it was police come to harass you, or it could be rogues masquerading as Sikh freedom fighters, come to ask for "donations". Expect they *weren't really asking, they were insisting, often at gunpoint.*

It was me that discovered the body the next morning; I used to come back from Vir Singh's house very early, at sunrise, to help milk the cows. I screamed at the top of my voice and your grandfather came running out. He...' His voice tailed off and he burst into tears. Sukhjeet had never seen his father like this and didn't know what to do. He wanted to get up and give him a hug but for some reason he remained frozen in his place, completely silent. Vir Singh squeezed his father's shoulder. That seemed to give him just enough strength to finish the story. *'He was covered in blood, naked apart from his shorts. His arms looked like they have been pulled out of their shoulder sockets. His face was so bruised and black you could hardly recognise him. Your grandfather's only words when he saw him were, "whatever is your will Vaheguru, we humbly accept"'.* His whole body shook as he wept, his head lowered, with Vir Singh patting his back to console him. And then, for what seemed like an eternity, nobody spoke. The continuous whirring of the air conditioning motor and Sukhjeet's father's forceful sobbing were the only noises in the sorrow filled room.

Sukhjeet impulsively lowered his gaze, unable to witness his father's distressed state and still inexplicably incapable of getting up and giving him a hug. His toes toyed with the frayed edges of the sizeable rug that formed the centrepiece of the room, concealing the otherwise bland marble floor and injecting some much need colour. Everything was pristinely clean as the room was only used when *'guests visited'*. Shelves proudly displayed framed family portraits and educational certificates as well as the multitude of sporting trophies Sukhjeet had accumulated. But the most prominent features were large paintings of Guru Nanak and Guru Gobind Singh, the first and last of the ten living Sikh gurus, respectively. Guru Nanak was painted, as was often the case, as someone who wouldn't hurt a fly; benevolence in his eyes, plump rosy cheeks and a white beard. A surprising depiction, Sukhjeet had always thought, given he single-handedly launched a revolutionary movement that challenged all societal discriminations of the time and took on the firmly entrenched, caste-ridden Hindu religious order head on. Guru Gobind Singh was painted more realistically, with wrathful eyes and adorned in weaponry. Probably a fair representation of someone who was forced to fight over thirteen battles to defend the Faith and who ultimately sacrificed his four young sons to the cause. The paintings hung on the wall, identical in size, in ornate wooden frames, each with a garland of flowers around them. The only person that came into the room routinely was Sukhjeet's mother, to supervise the cleaner and ensure she left it spotless but also to exchange the flowers with fresh garlands whenever they jaded. She would stand in from of them and recite a full 'Ardas' – prayer, each time she did so.

Snapping himself from his thoughts, back into the moment, Sukhjeet decided he need to try and move the conversation on. *'Didn't the police get investigated for that? Someone being killed in their custody?'*

Vir Singh answered, as his father was still clearly too moved by his recollections to continue conversing. *'Sukhi son, in those days, either the police would deny they had even arrested the individual in the first place. Or, like in your Joginder Chacha's case, they admitted they had arrested him as they wanted to claim the cash bounty for arresting a wanted "terrorist" but they said he tried to escape custody* and was killed in the firefight that ensued. An "encounter" they called it. Thousands of young men were killed by the police in this way, militants and innocents. Anyway, I said from the start, no point talking about these things. Just makes everyone upset. And for what? It doesn't matter now.'

'It matters.' Sukhjeet's retort was attention grab-bingly forceful, especially as he was normally so docile around elders. Both the men gave him their full atten-tion, looking up straight at him, Sukhjeet's father's face visibly wet. 'It matters to me. Daddy Ji was one hundred per-cent right uncle, we need to know. How else can my generation ensure this NEVER happens again?'

❖ ❖ ❖

7B. Wolverhampton, Eng-land: October 2016

'**M**y round, you got the coffees last three times,' Zainab insisted, as they walked out the class-room and towards the coffee machine.

'We could go for a drink somewhere else,' Sukhjeet suggested reticently, his voice trailing off towards the end of the sentence.

'Sure. Where you thinking?' Zainab stopped and

turned to face Sukhjeet, seemingly completely unphased by what was in his opinion a ground-breaking proposal. Surely, he had just asked her out on a date and she had explicitly accepted. He almost wished he had recorded it so she couldn't deny it later.

Encouraged by her enthusiastic response, Sukhjeet suddenly found his confidence and blasély recommended a nice-looking Indian restaurant he had often walked past on his way home from college.

'A restaurant? Just us two? Oh, I thought you were suggesting just a quick drink somewhere.' Zainab looked perturbed and she reached up and started nervously adjusting her headscarf.

Sukhjeet's face physically drooped. 'Oh, yes, sure, no, I meant, they have drinks there also. We don't have to eat.' The proposal made no sense and he knew it.

Then, as a much-needed lifeline, he noticed the edges of Zainab's lips upturn slightly, revealing the birth of a tiny smirk, before she quickly caved in and burst into fully fledged laughter, 'I am just messing with you; I would love to. J'adore Indian food. You can introduce me to some proper authentic Indian dishes.'

There was momentary annoyance at being teased during such a vulnerable moment, but soon enough, a cheery smile spread across Sukhjeet's face too.

'Welcome to "Punjab Karahi" sir, madam.' The short, smartly dressed waiter greeted them at the front door and led them to a table in the middle of the restaurant. In the far corner, a young, white couple were elatedly taking photographs of a giant, sizzling, smoking hotplate of meat that had just arrived on the table. Sukhjeet pointed out the hotplate to Zainab, the intensely flavoursome smoke of freshly barbequed meat and masalas wafting through his nostrils, suddenly stirring his hunger. Closer to them, an extended Indian family were sat on a table crammed with dishes of all varieties, the giant helium balloons giving away the occasion; grandma's eightieth birthday.

As they were being seated, Sukhjeet noticed the waiter looking closely at his steel bracelet, his Karra, a clear giveaway of his Sikh identity, before suspiciously examining Zainab's headscarf. He wasn't the only member of staff sizing them up. The barman, stood behind the wooden, purpose-built bar at one of the rear corners of the restaurant, was staring at them shamelessly, a completely gormless expression across his moustached face. He remained idle, clutching a wine glass in one hand and a towel in the other.

Their waiter spoke unnecessarily quickly, without pausing for a single breath. 'Please sir, madam, here are the menus. We have a fully licenced bar; beer, wine and spirits. Also, the food is one hundred percent NON-halal here. Would you like to order any drinks to start?'

Sukhjeet immediately looked towards Zainab, expecting her to hand the menu back, stand up and walk out the restaurant. What an idiot he was, bringing her to a non-halal restaurant. But she remained seated, cocking her head a little, in fact trying to decipher the reason for his own sudden, furrowed brow. 'You OK, something wrong?' she quizzed.

'It's not halal, it's OK for you?' He had no idea why he was leaning forward and whispering, the waiter was the one who had intentionally alerted them to this overlooked issue in the first place.

'Ha. I am vegetarian,' she responded, winking at

him cheekily. 'We still have a lot to learn about each other, eh? But you order whatever you want. Looked like you want that meat grill, judging by your excitement when we walked in?'

'No, I will eat vegetarian too. Let's share, that's how Indian food should be eaten. Then one day maybe you can take me to a Palestinian restaurant and introduce me to that?'

'Haven't seen many of those around Wolverhampton, have you? Don't worry, I will cook it for you.'

The waiter interrupted the conversation with a subtle cough, clearly keen to take both the order and his leave.

'Sukhi will order drinks. Order something really properly Indian.' It's the first time she had called him Sukhi, having only learned during the walk to the restaurant that this was how his family referred to him.

What he really wanted, to help calm his nerves a little, and something that was certainly 'properly Indian', was whiskey. Best not to push it though, he decided. 'Two lassis please.'

'Sweet or salty,' asked the waiter.

Zainab presented an excellent poker face. If she had a preference, she certainly wasn't giving it away. 'Both salty,' said Sukhjeet boldly, latching onto the empowerment of deciding for her. And then without warning, he followed, 'I will order food for us both now too.'

Throughout the ordering, Sukhjeet confirmed the Punjabi origin of each dish he was ordering and diligently explained to Zainab what each one consisted of. Meanwhile, Zainab sat with her elbow on the table, propping up her chin with her palm, attentively listening to the detailed descriptions, enjoying this assertive and indeed animated side of Sukhjeet that she was witnessing for the first time.

The conversation flowed naturally. Sukhjeet also began to open up a little but, as usual, Zainab led the way and shared detailed stories about her family and childhood.

'As a child, I just wanted to live life like normal kids I saw on TV, like in the American movies. To watch pop videos, dance, goof around, ride my bike on the streets.' Zainab paused to place a piece of naan into her mouth without letting the dark brown, soupy dhal drip. 'Sooo tasty. This dhal is to die for. I cannot believe you didn't learn the recipe from your mother before you left India.' Sukhjeet reflected on how little time he had when he left Punjab. Barely enough to say goodbye to his mother properly, never mind taking cooking lessons from her. Zainab waved her hand in front of her mouth before taking a gulp of water, 'but spicy,' she added to her previous comment belatedly. Sukhjeet could see small beads of perspiration starting to line her brow, along the edge of her headscarf.

'So, you couldn't do those things, because of the Israeli occupation you were explaining earlier?' Sukhjeet had been struggling to get his head around the complexity of the situation in Palestine and Israel, as explained by Zainab whilst crunching on poppadum earlier. The topic had been covered in his school history lessons but was generally portrayed as a conflict arising primarily from Islamic extremism, often drawing parallels to Pakistan sponsored terrorism in Indian administered Kashmir.

'Our village is in West Bank Area C. This area

belongs to my people but is occupied illegally by the Israelis. Every time you entered or left you had to queue in the baking sun, for hours sometimes, go through a checkpoint and have all your belongings searched. It was so demeaning. There were armed soldiers everywhere on the streets. It was too dangerous for us to be out and about, so, we just stayed home.' She paused for a gulp of her lassi, before continuing. 'It was as if there were two completely separate rule books. One for the Jewish settlers and one for the Arabs. Yet, to this day, my father has never spoken ill of Jews. "Jews are not bad, Arabs are not bad, but given half a chance, every human being is bad," is what he always used to say. We only have to look at our own history and how so many of our Palestinian leaders sold out time and time again, to see how true that is. The Jewish settlers were simply making the most the uneven playing field that was established for them. But the Israeli state, that is for sure responsible for the misfortune of so many Palestinians, and that really makes me rage.' She caught herself staring blankly past Sukhjeet, teleporting herself back to those dusty, sandy streets in her thoughts, and so consciously drew herself back into the moment. 'Anyway, back to my family's story. My father used to own a bakery in West Bank C but the Israeli authorities had it demolished.'

'How? Can they just do that?'

'The authorities wanted to build a residential area for Jewish settlers so they obtained a court order to demolish the bakery. Huge diggers came, accompanied by units of soldiers to make sure nobody could stop the work. And they kicked us off our own land...as if we were stray dogs. Just like that.'

'But surely they had to pay you the value of the

house?'

'They don't HAVE TO do anything Sukhi. That's how it works when you are under foreign rule. You have no right to expect rights.'

Sukhjeet only got as far as saying, 'but,' before Zainab cut in again.

'They paid for the value of the building itself, just the bricks. They didn't care that this was our livelihood. How was my father supposed to make a living? They had already taken our dignity and then they literally took the bread from our table as well.'

Sukhjeet was silent for a moment, his turn to day-dream this time, as he reflected on the injustices experienced by his own family. 'What did your father do?' he questioned in a quiet voice, gently stroking the scar on his cheek.

'STRUGGLE. FIGHT.' She slammed her fist on the table, sending scattered crumbs flying from the table-cloth into the air. Sukhjeet jumped in his seat, stunned by this sudden aggression. The intensity of her fury genuinely surprised him; he had no idea she had such rage buried inside her. She continued, 'like my people have done for generations and will continue to do until we are liberated.' Creases had appeared on her forehead, running up from the top of her nose, between her pristinely manicured eyebrows, and reaching almost to her headscarf. The birthday grandma looked over from her table, even putting down her gulab jamun desert to ensure she wouldn't miss any part of what she hoped would be a Bollywood drama style, domestic, marital dispute showdown.

Eventually, Zainab lowered her voice, having also noted the attention they were now attracting. The initial forceful whispering soon elevated in volume though, as her emotions once again got the better of her. 'My father used part of the money to send my brother to France and put some aside so I could follow a few years later when I was old enough and my brother had cleared the way. Once us kids were safely out of the country, he gave most of the rest to the resistance movement – Hamas. When we were desperate, they were the ones that had given us money to feed and clothe ourselves. He has been arrested three times now but, in the end, they always have to release him because they cannot actually prove he donated to Hamas and still does.' Zainab paused to take a drink of water, emptying the last drops out of her glass. Sukhjeet could see her welling up and she tried to subtly wipe the corner of her eye with the base of her thumb. Sukhjeet, not knowing what to do, waved the empty jug at the waiter, prompting him to take it away and refill it. 'Isn't life crazy?' she blurted out, letting out a little laugh even though tears were now starting to stream down her cheek. 'My father spent his whole life warning my brother against getting involved with Hamas, calling them trouble-makers and extremists. He supported Fatah and their attempts to negotiate diplomatically, both directly with Israel and through the UN. But where does that get you? Nowhere. Bullies don't negotiate with the weak. You have to be strong and you have to fight. The world will call you terrorists but fuck them.' She picked up her napkin to wipe her cheek, having given up trying to conceal the fact that she was in tears. 'Sorry, I am probably not making much sense.'

Sukhjeet leaned over and grabbed her hand with both of his as she went to put the napkin back on the table. He considered reaching up to wipe the remaining tears from her cheeks for her, but thought better of it, especially with the grandma still glancingly unapprovingly in their direction every few minutes. Zainab looked straight at him, a little taken aback, but not sufficiently so to make her impulsively withdraw her hand. And then time stood still, as they looked into each other's eyes. Hers were truly a sight to behold. He had wondered on a few occasions whether they were coloured contact lenses, until she settled his internal debate by mentioning in passing that everyone in her family said she had inherited her eyes from her paternal grandmother, who had passed away before Zainab was born. They were an intricate, emerald green mosaic, a million little tiles arranged perfectly into a circle, with a slight auburn tinge closest to the pupil. It was impossible not to be mesmerised when you saw them close up.

'It makes sense to me.' The sheer intensity with which Sukhjeet said those words was unmistakable and the genuineness of his sentiment poured out. However, he wanted to be yet more explicit. 'I understand absolutely everything you are saying, from the bottom of my heart I understand it, Zainab. I know how you feel.' He felt her fingers clasp tightly onto his hands and with those eyes alone she somehow managed to ask him why he was so closed about his own story and whether he would ever let her in to his past. 'I will tell you everything Zainab, just give me some time,' he replied, out loud.

SECTION 8: BEING HEARD

'To live is to suffer, to survive is to find some meaning in the suffering.' Friedrich Nietzsche.

8A. Amritsar, Punjab: Jan 2015

'*B*rothers, sisters, today was our third meeting since we embarked on this endeavour at the start of the academic year. Each time we meet, the numbers are swelling. Today, we have counted over seventy attendees assembled here.'

'He will be eternally blessed who says...!' This first part of the Sikh victory exultation was shouted out loudly by a member of the audience, sat near the back but easily identifiable by his arm being raised high into the air as he spoke.

The customary response was bellowed back heartily in unison by everyone else, '...God is the eternal truth!'.

Encouraged, Sukhjeet continued. 'We need to be crystal clear about our mission. We will not let those in chairs of power create divisions in our communities based on religion. We have Sikh, Hindu. Muslim and Christian students in this group and all of us are committed to one goal. And that is to unveil the truth about the recent, dark history of Punjab and transparently record it for posterity, so we can ensure that this can never happen to us again. Never again can innocent men and women be picked up by police and the army and then "disappeared", or killed in "encounters". Never again can...'

'Quick! Everyone! Three police jeeps have just come through the main gates of the campus. Run! Get out!' The messenger was already completely out of breath from his sprint but as soon as he finished yelling the warning, he darted back out the canteen, energised by adrenalin. Immediately, complete chaos erupted in the room.

Sukhjeet tried desperately to restore calm, shouting into the microphone in an effort to be heard over the commotion of chairs being knocked over and a general exodus towards the door. 'Brothers and sisters, there is no need to be afraid and run. We have done nothing wrong or illegal. Listen to me. We are stronger if we all stick together.' His attempts were futile; the room was emptying fast. Anita, though undoubtedly alarmed, her heart racing and breathing quickening, remained determined not to succumb to panic and instead act rationally and usefully. She started to frantically but diligently sweep up every one of the information sheets they were planning to distribute after the event and stuff them roughly into her cloth shoulder bag.

Then, just as the last of the students were squeezing out of the door, they found themselves opposed by a tide of khaki uniforms pushing them back into the canteen. The policemen entered the room with determined force, all wearing deadpan facial expressions and clutching intimidating, wooden batons in their hand. However, they didn't stop the students from filtering around the troop and back out the doors behind them. Clearly, they had a singular target in their sights. And stood on the makeshift stage with a microphone in his hand, Sukhjeet was not difficult to identify.

Last to enter was the inspector, who strolled in nonchalantly at the tail end of the police troop and took up position a few feet short of Sukhjeet. He was a tall, broad-shouldered, bearded man, with a large paunch that hung over his thick leather belt, partly concealing the oversized metal buckle. Despite the mild temperatures outside, sweat patches spread out from his armpits all the way to the name badge pinned onto the breast of his khaki uniform; 'Inspector Baldev Singh Punjab Police'. After a momentary silence and having looked Sukhjeet directly in the eyes, he shouted loudly to his constable, 'handcuff him. Let's get him to the station and then we will discuss human rights campaigning with him over a nice, hot cup of tea.'

Anita stepped towards the inspector and screamed, 'please, don't arrest him, he hasn't done anything wrong. Please.' Inspector Baldev Singh turned to face Anita and without any warning he raised his arm and slapped her face so violently that she tumbled onto the floor, sliding a good few metres along the smooth tiles before coming to a stop. The sound of the impact echoed seemingly endlessly around the cavernous room. Without any regard for Anita, who was lying dazed and in complete shock, Baldev Singh reached up to adjust his sizeable turban, the vigour of the blow having unseated it a little.

Sukhjeet jolted forward but was restrained by two of the constables, each pulling one of his arms behind his back. *'You bastard, leave her alone,'* he shouted.

'Bastard?' Baldev Singh let out a loud bellowing laugh. *'I will respond to that at the station,'* he said eventually, once he had regained his composure. He started twirling his moustache and looking around at his constables, who had also started smiling in appeasement. Turning his attention back to Sukhjeet, he continued. *'Now, you keep your mouth shut until I ask you to speak.'* He took a further step towards his prisoner, now standing menacingly within striking distance. *'But when I do ask you to speak, you best answer my questions very clearly, or you are going to regret it.'*

'You cannot arrest me, I haven't done anything wrong. What is the charge? Where is the warrant?'

Baldev Singh grabbed the microphone from Sukhjeet's hand and smashed it into his left temple with all his might. Sukhjeet immediately slumped forward. He would have completely collapsed onto the floor had the constables not been restraining him. He even lost his vision momentarily, replaced by a bright, white explosion of light. The sensory overload was completely debilitating and his ears pounded with a high-pitched squeal for hours after the strike. The violence achieved its intended effect. Sukhjeet fell silent, only vaguely aware of what was happening to him. He was led out the canteen, without any idea how hard Anita was screaming in the background. Bundled aggressively into the back of a police jeep parked incongruously on the manicured lawn outside the canteen, he was soon on his way to Inspector Baldev Singh's station.

Having sat in the corner of the prison cell for some hours, Sukhjeet was especially struggling with the stench, even more so than the thumping headache. He tried burying his nose inside his t-shirt but this didn't really help. Raw human sewage clogged the squat toilet in the corner and hordes of flies were buzzing around the cell as a result. He was sharing the ten feet by ten feet room with four others, all of whom looked like they had been there for days. One was in particularly poor condition and lay idle, too weak to brush off the sizeable cockroaches crawling all over him. Sukhjeet had tried to start a conversation with the others by whisperingly asking if the sick prisoner was OK. He received only blank stares in response, apart from the older, turbaned, Sikh prisoner who had put his hands together in a 'it's in God's hands' gesture. The cell door had opened only once during the time Sukhjeet had been there. It was not lost on Sukhjeet that as soon as the prisoners heard the key entering the door, the three who were still mobile had immediately retreated, crawling into a huddle near the back corner. Fortunately, that time it had only been delivery of a tray of plain rice that was dumped in the middle of the cell for them all to share.

The next time keys entered the door, the reason wasn't so benign. A golden orange, dusky sunlight suddenly fanned out across the cell as the door creaked open. Sukhjeet quickly concluded that he must have been there for around seven hours since he was arrested around noon. Inspector Baldev Singh stood at the open door, flanked by two constables, the shorter one clutching a large ring of keys. *'This one,'* said Baldev Singh, pointing at Sukhjeet, *'he was a bit hot earlier, cool him down for me. I will come back after dinner to formally question him.'*

Sukhjeet was then handcuffed and dragged out the cell. He didn't resist, there was no point. He simply closed his eyes and listened. He heard the clicking of Baldev's Singh's shoes getting ever quieter as he strolled off down the corridor, and the murmured prayers of the old Sikh prisoner, *'Vaheguru, be merciful on this poor boy'.*

It was four of them in the end, sometimes taking turns and sometimes joining forces to torment him. He was stripped to his shorts, knocked to the ground, kicked, punched, thrashed with thick electrical cables and flogged with a leather belt. His loud cries for help and mercy soon turned into whimpers. Just as his body started to numb to the pain, they changed tactic. Gathering up his limp torso from the ground, one grabbed his arms behind his back whilst two others kneeled down, grabbing one leg each and pulling them apart with all their might. Sukhjeet squealed, sounding more like a distressed animal than a human, for he was in too much pain to scream normally. *'Mother-fucker! Was acting the big man earlier, weren't you? Now, already pissed yourself like a little girl. Now talk you bastard.'* With that, the one policeman that was still standing kicked Sukhjeet in the groin with full force. Sukhjeet passed out.

Time lost all meaning and indeed relevance, replaced by only pain and fear. As a drunk Inspector Baldev Singh frantically scanned around the cell, Sukhjeet's experiences from the last few hours flashed before him. Being cocooned on the floor trying to protect himself against the blows raining down on him...finding himself suspended by ropes from a hook in the ceiling...being tormented by Baldev Singh...the head-butt.

'I am sorry. Sorry. Please, please, let me go. I haven't done anything wrong'. Tears were starting to well in Sukhjeet's eyes. 'I beg you, let me go. I am like your little brother'. The words fell on deaf ears. As Baldev Singh marched towards him, Sukhjeet could see something in his hand, but couldn't quite make out what it was.

'Mother-fucker, you called me a bastard and I let it go. Now you have the gall to strike me? You will pay for this.' He raised the rusty screwdriver high into the air and plunged it with brutal force into Sukhjeet's left cheek. Even before Sukhjeet could scream, he had wrenched it back out and plunged it in again, this time also pulling sideways maniacally, tearing Sukhjeet's cheek open between the two entry holes. 'Now talk. Come on, talk you sister fucker!' Baldev's shouting had gotten the attention of the constables who ran in and physically pulled the enraged inspector off Sukhjeet. 'Sir, no, you cannot do this, please sir. The principal of the university and the boy's father have lobbied some municipality members and they are applying for bail. We need to be careful.'

Warm blood was gushing into Sukhjeet's throat and he was having to consciously take big gulps and keep swallowing in order to keep his throat clear for breathing, for his nose was already broken and completely clogged with congealed plasma and bone fragments. This deliberate breathing effort, adrenalin racing around his veins and initial shock, all temporarily distracted him from the excruciating pain, but not for long.

8B. Wolverhampton, England: November 2016

What was planned for tonight was definitely a date, of the romantic variety. Sukhjeet had left no room for any doubt or confusion in Zainab's mind. The instant he had asked her if she 'wanted to go out' with him, he had realised that it sounded childish but having thought about it extensively since, he still wasn't sure what else he could have said or done. Just asked her if she wanted to go for dinner again? Surely that would have left her wondering whether this was just another casual bite to eat 'as friends', just like the curry night? Or, maybe he could have leant in for a kiss without saying anything, like he had seen in Western movies. That's what he desperately wanted to do but he couldn't pluck up the courage. Anyway, her headscarf suggested she wasn't 'that type' of girl, though she had casually mentioned previous boyfriends. The only thing that ultimately mattered though, was that his method had worked. Zainab had smirked, amused by his undeniably immature choice of words no doubt, raised one of her hands, touching her palm to her cheek, cocked her head slightly and said, 'I would love to.'

Unsurprisingly for a Saturday afternoon, the town centre was a hive of activity. Teenage boys were goofing around outside McDonalds, chasing each other up and down the thoroughfare. Teenage girls in tight, lycra leggings and puffer jackets strutted past the boys, looping back around repeatedly, pretending not to be interested in the flagrant attention they attracted each time they did so. Dozens of pushchairs with shopping bags hanging off every hook and handle were being expertly manoeuvred past each other like dodgems. Wafts of fresh doughnuts, hot-dogs and frying onions filled the air.

Sukhjeet was intent on remaining focused as he was rapidly running out of time. He wanted to get his shopping done, return home, iron his clothes, bathe and trim his beard before meeting Zainab that evening. However, buying a new outfit for his date was proving harder than expected. A pair of Levi jeans and a shirt would cost him over a hundred pounds and he couldn't bring himself to spend that. He opted to heed Preetam's advice and try somewhere called 'Primark', where clothes were apparently cheap but looked the part and were sure to *'help him get laid'*.

When he arrived, the store was a scene of absolute chaos. Clear evidence that it had been relentlessly busy all day, piles of clothing lay strewn on the floor, discarded by earlier shoppers and not yet placed back onto hangers by the staff. Frenzied crowds waded through the heaps, some actually crawling on their hands and knees. Obsessively scouring the aisles, hunting for their own size amongst the bargain items, they had been drawn in by the huge, bright red 'Up To 50% Off' signs plastering the windows.

How different this was to his previous life. Though not overly affluent by any means, he was nevertheless accustomed to visiting designer emporiums in the cities of Amritsar and Chandigarh and being waited on hand-and-foot by eager shop assistants during his regular clothes shopping excursions with Satwant. Priding themselves on staying abreast of the latest fashion trends, he and his friends had always lived by the spirit of the chorus from one of their favourite bhangra songs; *'Hair styled, ready to flirt, wearing shades from Armani and a Tommy Hilfiger shirt.'*

Sukhjeet was stirred from his daydream by a loud, shrieky, 'excuse me gorgeous', as he was gently nudged aside by a plump, busty blonde, clearly determined to reach the mini-skirts aisle as quickly as possible. Eventually managing to escape the expansive ladies' clothes section, he found his way to the men's area which thankfully seemed a little more ordered. Thirty minutes later, he was walking out of the store with new, grey jeans, a thick, white, cotton shirt and a pair of tan, leather loafers, all for under fifty pounds.

It had been Zainab's suggestion to meet at Pizza Express. They both arrived at almost exactly the same time and to Sukhjeet's delight, it was clear that Zainab had also made a real effort. Most striking was her headscarf; pink chiffon with a tasteful but audacious flowery print. She removed her long winter coat and folded it over, placing it carefully on the sofa bench lining the wall. Immediately, she plonked herself sat down next to it, 'shotgun, I get the comfy seat.' She was wearing a long, grey jumper dress that extended down to her mid-thigh, with a wide belt that was tightly buckled around her thin waist. Sukhjeet's eyes started tracking along the outline of her perfect figure, which her outfit unapologetically flaunted. The neck line was lower than he had ever seen before, though still quite conservative, and he could see a simple necklace with rose coloured stones that complemented her headscarf perfectly, as did the varnish on her immaculately manicured nails. Her lipstick was brighter than usual and Sukhjeet found himself pausing fixatedly on her face, struggling to shift his gaze even though he was well aware he was staring. 'You OK? Sit down, will you? My neck will start hurting if I have to keep looking up at you like this,' Zainab giggled.

'You look, errmm, very nice today.' He should have said something stronger than 'very nice'. 'Beautiful' or 'stunning' perhaps. But the moment was gone. Unable to cope with even the five second silence that ensued, he followed up with, 'I really like your headscarf.'

'Thanks. Hijab.'

'Sorry?'

'Hijab. It's called a hijab. Headscarf is what posh French women wear!' Zainab smiled and then gave Sukhjeet a quick but intentionally obvious look up and down. 'You brush up quite well yourself,' she remarked, following up with one of those cheeky winks that he adored so much.

Sukhjeet took off his own jacket and threw it coolly on top of hers, whilst taking a seat opposite. It was then Zainab's turn to lose herself a little whilst taking a good look at Sukhjeet. He really was a very handsome man. She admired him unashamedly; the new haircut, the freshly tidied beard that accentuated his sharp jaw-line, fitted shirt with the top few buttons undone and straining slightly at the chest, and rolled up sleeves showing muscular forearms. He knew he was being examined and instinctively raised his arm, ostensibly to scratch his forehead but actually partly to flex his biceps and partly intended to hide his scar, which was more exposed today since he trimmed his beard.

'Sukhjeet, how did you get that scar?' Zainab was astute enough to piece together that the scar was linked to his slight limp and that all the evasiveness about his past was somehow tied in with these injuries. She saw the look on his face and instantly regretted asking the question. 'Sorry, I haven't even asked you how your week was. Silly old inquisitive me, prying as normal. Let's talk about something...'

Sukhjeet interrupted her mid-sentence. 'It's OK Zainab, I will tell you everything.' And after unashamedly ordering himself a double whiskey, he did. His life in the Punjab, his family, Anita, his uncle's fate, his own political awakening, the arrest, the deal that was struck with the police, his harrowing journey to England. His early experiences at various West Midlands building sites. His immigration status. He told her absolutely everything. And Zainab listened, attentively.

They eventually walked out of the restaurant some three hours later. Almost immediately, Zainab linked her arm with Sukhjeet's. It was neither particularly surprising nor awkward; it just felt right. They walked slowly down the quiet street, largely in silence, Zainab leaning her head on Sukhjeet's shoulder.

'I will walk you home. It's late for you to be travelling alone.' Sukhjeet knew Zainab lived about ten minutes walking distance from the town centre, in the opposite direction to his house.

'You really don't have to. Anyway, you live in Blakenhall, that's the opposite way.'

'I am not going to let you go home alone at eleven at night Zainab. You don't have a choice.'

She looked up at Sukhjeet just as they happened to be walking under a street lamp. Yellow sodium lamp light illuminated her face. She was smiling, though he could see her mascara had smudged a little from the tears she had shed listening to his story earlier. 'OK, thank you.'

They walked in silence, neither of them wanting to disturb the magic of the moment. Vaporous clouds floated in front of their faces as they exhaled into the chilly air. Zainab snuggled tighter against Sukhjeet in a futile attempt to ward off the cold and they quickened their pace to get home as quickly as possible. Suddenly, just as they turned a corner, Zainab felt Sukhjeet tug her into the road as he abruptly changed course to cross over the road. Looking up, she saw two young, black men approaching about a hundred yards away, the only sign of life in an otherwise completely deserted street. By the time she had worked out what was going through Sukhjeet's head, they were on the opposite pavement.

'What's up?' she quizzed, feigning naivety.

'Nothing.'

'Why did we cross the road suddenly?'

'Oh, just, there were some people coming on that side.'

'Some people?'

'Yes. Best to be safe, never know with….'

'With what? Black guys?'

'Just don't want trouble.'

'Sukhjeet, that is an absolutely awful way to think.'

'Come on, we know what they are like.'

'They? Wow!' Zainab abruptly stopped walking and yanked her arm away, immediately thrusting her now free hand into her jacket pocket. She took a step to make some distance between them before turning to directly face Sukhjeet, who was still catching up with the turn of events. 'For someone who has spent the last three hours telling me about all the racist abuse you have got in the UK since you moved here, you haven't developed much empathy for others have you?'

'Crossing the road isn't racism. I didn't say anything to them.'

'Having a prejudice against people because of how their skin colour is THE definition of racism.'

'Zainab, please, lower you voice.'

'No. I won't. They are criminals because they are black. You should be a geeky, hardworking shopkeeper or IT guy because you are Indian. And I am a fucking terrorist because I am a Muslim. Isn't that racism?

'Zainab, you are misunderstanding me.' But from the strength of her reaction he knew there was no fruitful discussion to be had on the topic, so he opted to simply apologise instead. 'I...I am sorry...I shouldn't have...'

Zainab started to work off and Sukhjeet tried to follow. She spoke whilst walking away from him. 'No. I am going to walk alone. Just because I am a woman, doesn't mean I constantly need a man next to me for my safety. Though I guess you hold that prejudice as well.'

'Zainab, just let me walk you home, please?'

Whilst continuing to walk off at a determined pace, shaking her head as she went, Zainab replied. 'Go home Sukhjeet.' And then after a painful thirty second silence, she threw him a lifeline. 'Think about what I said. See you in college on Thursday.' With that, she turned a corner and was gone. A misty trail and ever quieter footsteps were all that remained as Sukhjeet stood silent and alone.

'Everything alright bro? You OK yeah?' Sukhjeet turned around towards the deep male voice behind him. It was the shorter black man calling out, with a thick, unmistakeable West African accent.

'Yeah, fine thanks,' replied Sukhjeet, lying profusely.

'Cool man. You were just standing there staring into space. Just checking you didn't need any help. Best get home before you freeze, my friend.'

'Yeah, thanks. Sure, I was just going.'

'Come on Godwin, let's go man. I am freezin' my nuts off here,' said the taller man, as he stood blowing warm breath into his cupped hands. Godwin obliged and within seconds the duo disappeared into a multi storey car park.

SECTION 9:
DISTANT LANDS

'We cannot control the wind, but we can adjust the sails.' Thomas Monson.

9A. Tarn Tarn, Punjab: Feb 2015

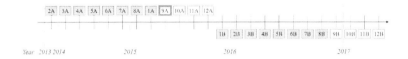

S ukhjeet sat silently opposite his father in their living room, listening to his mother's footsteps as she paced frantically around his bedroom upstairs. Summoning up all his willpower to overcome the acute lethargy he was feeling since being released from hospital, Sukhjeet started sullenly climbing the marble clad staircase, clutching onto the bannisters for support. Within a few steps he was wheezing and had to stop off half way up for a few moments to catch his breath, before continuing to plod slowly on. He had just taken his daily dose of painkillers and antibiotics and the cocktail flowed through his veins, weighing him down debilitatingly but having yet little beneficial impact on the searing ache across the entire left side of his face.

Having spent a night in hospital after his discharge from prison, Sukhjeet had been home five days now. His release had been arranged by his father a few hours after the episode in the interrogation cell, but only after agreeing to a punishing financial deal with Baldev Singh.

The first two days were a complete haze, spent with Sukhjeet lying comatose in bed, drugged up, sweating and nauseous from both the drugs and the nightmarish memories of his incarceration that just kept on swirling around in his head. The next few days were better, especially once he was again able to start eating solids. With age on his side, his recovery was progressing undeniably quickly but the ongoing difficulty of simple feats like ascending the stairs continually served to remind him how much of a weakened state he was still in.

Through the ajar bedroom door, he saw most of his wardrobe of designer clothes laid out across the bed, as his mother diligently but rapidly folded the items and laid them out in a neat pile, that was already considerably larger than the open suitcase on the floor. *'Mom.'* There was no response. *'Mom, there is no point. The agent said on the phone that I should only take a small rucksack. It's fine, I will be in England in a few weeks and I can buy some new clothes there.'*

'How do they expect you to go for weeks on end, across all those cold countries, with only one rucksack?'

'Mom, it's nearly spring time, the weather will be fine. Come, let's sit together downstairs.'

'But...'

'Mom...'

'Just let me pack a few more...'

Sukhjeet walked over, pulled his sweater from his mother's arms and threw his arms around her. After desperately trying to resist her emotions for a moment, she leaned into his chest and broke down into a torrent of barely audible tears. He could feel her holding onto him ever more tightly, as if she would collapse in a heap if he wasn't there to physically support her. In actual fact, she was just ensuring that nothing could take him away from her, at least for these precious few minutes.

A short while later, Sukhjeet headed back downstairs to find that Vir Singh had arrived and was in the midst of handing large elasticated bundles of cash to Sukhjeet's father.

'Sat Sri Akal Uncle Ji.'

Vir Singh put the notes down and looked up at Sukhjeet. *'Sat Sri Akal son. Has is your cheek? Bleeding stopped? Stiches holding up? Your father was saying they used these new dissolving ones?'*

'Yes. Can still taste a little blood but much less.'

'How is the pain?'

'Pain is OK with the tablets.' It wasn't entirely untrue; the drugs were finally starting to work their magic.

'We must thank God. When He is on your side, nobody can harm you. At least we got you out of there before that butcher Baldev Singh...'

Sukhjeet's father cut Vir Singh off with a loud cough, before he was able to finish his sentence. Vir Singh understood and let Sukhjeet's father change the subject. *'Vir Singh Ji was able to get hold of all the cash we need to pay the travel agent tonight.'* The title 'travel agent' gave the man an air of legitimacy that Sukhjeet strongly felt was undeserved.

'And the bribery money you promised Baldev Singh?' Sukhjeet quizzed, unable to avoid stressing the word *'bribery'.* Though it still ached acutely when he spoke, he was determined not to let the pain stop him from talking to his family during the last night he would spend with them for a very long time. Deep down, he knew full well it might even be the very last time he would ever see them. But neither he nor his parents could cope with that dire prospect, so everyone had settled with reconciling themselves to 'potentially quite a long time apart.'

'We will need to sell land for that which will take some time. That crook, Inspector Baldev Singh, has agreed to wait. After all, where can we really run to whilst indebted to him. He certainly isn't worried about getting his money. And at that point we also will repay the creditors from whom Vir Singh has borrowed the cash to pay the travel agent's fees.'

Vir Singh was nodding in agreement. *'There are a few local men who are prepared to buy the land right now but they have gotten wind that we are in a difficult situation with the police and are trying to take advantage by offering very low rates. I will look for someone from further afield. I know a man in Ludhiana who deals with investors from as far afield as Delhi and even Bombay.'*

The 'travel agent' arrived exactly at the agreed time. Sukhjeet reflected how even Indians could be punctual when there was hard cash to be collected. Shivjot Kumar was a short, stocky, bald man. Thick, black glasses rested low on his nose and he wore an ill-fitting, blue, nautical themed shirt that partly hung out of his trousers in a generally dishevelled fashion. He walked into the living room clutching a battered, brown, leather brief-case, complaining in quite a formal, urban Hindi dialect about the poor state of the roads and the root cause being government corruption. The irony of a human trafficker protesting about law-breaking was not lost on Sukhjeet and had his cheek not hurt so much it may have even elicited a smirk from him. The agent then started to explain the deal and how it would work, making the effort to speak in Punjabi this time. *'Why don't you start on dinner?'* Sukhjeet's father suggested to his mother, wanting to spare her the potential trauma of listening to what her beloved son may have to endure over the next few weeks. She replied in an uncharacteristically defiant tone that surprised both Sukhjeet and his father.

'No. I am going to listen to what the agent is promising and make sure he knows I will personally come and interrogate him good and proper if he doesn't deliver my son safely.'

'Dear sister, there is nothing to worry about. Everything is in safe hands.' Shivjot was perspiring lightly, despite the fact that it was the middle of winter and everyone else was sat in shawls and sweaters to stay warm. Sukhjeet's mother stood up and turned on the ceiling fan for his sole comfort. Appreciative of the gesture, he went on to explain that the deluxe package had been purchased for Sukhjeet and described what this meant. Normally, the price for such a package would have been fifteen lakhs (1,500,000 Rupees, equivalent to $21,000) but in this case it was twenty-five lakhs (2,500,000 Rupees, equivalent to $35,000) given the extremely short notice. He also explained how proud he was to have made these arrangements so quickly but conceded that they should be *'grateful to God that his team had a spare passport'* from a specific case that had fallen through only this week as that particular family was ultimately unable to raise the requisite funds.

Sukhjeet stared up at the fan blades whizzing around, reflecting on how much 'thanking of God' everyone felt was due whereas in his opinion, if anything, God owed them all a serious explanation right now. His pondering was interrupted by an Indian passport being thrust into his hands by the agent. It looked well used and contained official immigration stamps from various Asian countries as well as one from Russia. He flicked to the back page where a relatively recent photo of him was perfectly fixed under the laminate. 'Sukhjeet Singh Gill'; correct apart from the intentionally false surname 'Gill'.

'Let me see, son.' Sukhjeet obligingly passed the document to his father, who went to examine it intimately, testing the laminate to ensure it wouldn't peel away from any of the corners and checking whether all the visa stickers were securely affixed. After a few moments of scrutiny, he handed it to Vir Singh, nodding in approval.

'It's first class, sir.' The agent resumed his evidently well-rehearsed patter, whilst the passport continued to circulate, eventually ending up back with Sukhjeet. If the agent was to be believed, the plan was well trodden and entirely fool-proof. Sukhjeet would catch a flight from New Delhi to Moscow the following night, on the pretence of visiting a specialist Russian hospital for treatment of a skin condition. The slightly bloodied gauze dressing on his cheek would only further support the referral letter from one of the top hospitals in Punjab. This letter, stamped multiple times to prove its authenticity, along with an Aeroflot Airlines flight ticket, was passed to Sukhjeet by the agent, who then abruptly switched to addressing his 'customer' in English. 'Please be noting that the return flight sector is actually already can-

celled but for purposes of immigration officer inspection in Moscow you can show him this return portion of the ticket no problem.'

'*Check everything properly Sukhjeet, I have heard so many stories about these agents doing a shoddy job with documents and then running off with all their so called "customer's" money.*' Sukhjeet's mother's remark was aimed directly at the agent who was looking increasing uncomfortable, crossing and uncrossing his stumpy legs every few seconds.

'*Looks fine from what I can tell, mom.*'

'*Dear sister, I fully understand your apprehension, but please trust me. I take personal responsibility for getting your son to England. You have my number; you can call me anytime if there is any problem.*'

'*Time will tell,*' Sukhjeet's mother remarked under her breath, her furrowed brow and tight lips unequivocally revealing that she remained entirely unconvinced. '*Explain the rest of the plan please. What happens after Sukhi arrives in Moscow?*' Both Sukhjeet's father and Vir Singh, though clearly surprised by the direct manner with which Sukhjeet's mother was engaging with the agent, seemed happy enough to let her take the lead.

The agent cleared his throat and took a gulp from the glass of water that had been placed in front of him. '*Sukhjeet will first clear immigration in Moscow. This will be no problem as we have the passport with legitimate medical visit visa. After that, it is quite straightforward. Our local agent will meet Sukhjeet outside the airport and then he will be transported across Europe in trucks.*' He turned to face Sukhjeet directly. '*Sukhjeet Ji, remember to give this passport to our local agent once he meets you. He will then destroy it. An Indian passport is only a liability for you from that point.*' By the time he returned to address Sukhjeet's mother, he found her lost in her own thoughts, staring intently at the floor. He spoke to her anyway, hoping to draw her back into the moment. '*The only complicated bit is the entry into England. They have built a tunnel under the sea all the way from France to England. These Britishers – very clever people, they have the best engineers, no surprise they ruled the entire world.*' Sukhjeet's mother looked up with a stern expression, prompting the agent to terminate his digression. '*Err. Sorry. So, what was I saying? Yes, so, in this tunnel they have scanners that can detect any humans in a truck, just from their body heat. But please don't worry, Sukhjeet Ji will be given some special "thermal" blankets that he can wrap himself in. Also, with this deluxe package, the truck driver will be one of our regulars and will make sure everything runs smoothly. You see, with the standard package the boys have to make their own way across, so they hide in trucks without the driver even knowing they are there. Sukhjeet won't have this problem. Once in UK, our local agent there will give him a fake British passport and driving licence. He cannot use it for anything official, but it is OK for showing to any casual employers, landlords, colleges or anyone that just wants to see you have a right to stay in UK.*'

Further administrative details were exchanged and when the time came to hand over the plastic bag bulging with cash, Sukhjeet's mother stood up. '*Brother, would you like to eat something, I am about to heat up dinner.*' It was a parting, affectionate gesture. After all, this stranger seemingly had the power of life and death over her son and she was keen to end her encounter with him on good terms.

'*No sister, I best be heading off soon, it's getting late.*'

'*OK.*' She raised her two hand together in the customary manner and said, 'Sat Sri Akal brother,' to the agent. However, there was also a heartfelt plea embedded in the action and further conveyed silently with her expressive eyes. It was not lost on anyone in the room.

The agent stood up, clutching his own hands together to return the farewell greeting. 'Sat Sri Akal. And... sister, please don't worry about Sukhjeet. He will be fine.' Sukhjeet's mother nodded and with that she backed out of the room, her hands remaining clasped together throughout.

Shortly after dinner, Vir Singh also made his excuses and left the family to themselves, promising to return in the morning in case there was anything more he could help with. The others returned back to the living room, all three clutching metal cups of steaming hot milk with both hands. Sukhjeet's mother spoke first. 'I have put extra cardamom in to help everyone sleep. And yours has a big dollop of honey too Sukhi. It will act as an antiseptic for your mouth.'

Sukhjeet didn't want to go. He didn't want to leave his parents, his home, his friends, his life, his Anita. However, expressing this sentiment was out of the question. He needed to be strong for his parents' sake. It was bad enough losing a son but knowing how disheartened he himself was about leaving, would break them. But he couldn't help himself from exploring whether this drastic measure was absolutely, strictly necessary. 'Daddy ji, how much of our land will we need to sell to pay Baldev Singh?'

'About a third of it, some 3 acres, if we can achieve a fair sale price of around 40 lakhs (4,000,000 Rupees, equivalent to $56,000) per acre. Baldev Singh wants one crore (100

115

lakhs, which is 10,000,000 Rupees, equivalent to $140,000)
and then we also need to pay Vir Singh the agent fees so he can
return whatever he has borrowed for us.'

'*A third?'* Sukhjeet looked surprised. They were by
no means the largest landowners in the area but they
had never been wanting of anything growing up and they
owed that to their land. It was strange to imagine that
a third of what had provided such a privileged lifestyle
would be gone in one foul swoop.

'*The land and all our possessions aren't ours anyway.*
They have always been on loan and the time has come to re-
turn some of them.'

Sukhjeet looked at his father, surprised at what he
initially thought was the start of some startling revelation. However, his father's posture revealed the actual
underlying point he was making. He was sat looking up
towards the ceiling, holding up his glass of milk as a sym-
bolic further offering. '*Nothing within me is mine, every-*
thing belongs to You. If I surrender to You what is already
Yours, then what has it cost me?'

Sukhjeet's mother responded to his father's quotation from the Sikh holy texts with '*Vaheguru, Vaheguru'*
under her breath.

Sukhjeet quickly brought the conversation back
to practicalities. '*So, once we pay off Baldev Singh, your*
view is that he would continue to harass us? Is that really the
case? Surely, the charges would have been dropped?'

'*The problem is that the original charge was one of se-*
dition – "offences against the State". Baldev Singh did that to
ensure we could not get you released on bail. The lawyer told
us it wasn't even worth wasting our time trying that avenue
to get you out. So, firstly, that snake would have "harassed"
you sufficiently in jail to extract a confession.' Sukhjeet's

father chose his words carefully, softening third-degree torture to *'harassment'*. *'Then, even with that confession, the trial would have lasted many years whilst you rotted in jail. The only way to avoid all this was to pay off Baldev Singh and hence he could demand any sum he wanted. We had no leverage at all. However, all he is doing is releasing you without charge due to a lack of evidence. But history bears witness to the fact that there is no such thing as ever being a truly free man in this country, once you have been even suspected of sedition. Baldev Singh will get greedy again soon enough and come back to extort more by pinning something on you.'* His father then went on to repeat the overall plan. *'So, we need to get you out of India as quickly as possible without any of his local spies hearing about it. The story will be that you just vanished one night. The CID might tap our phones after that so you cannot call us until it all quietens down. Like I said before, your mother and I suggest two full years or so. Anyway, we will get a message directly from the agent confirming you arrived OK.'*

'Of course, he will arrive OK.' Sukhjeet's mother was speaking to herself but unintentionally loud enough for everyone to hear.

'But if I kept myself to myself, then on what basis would the police come back for me?' Sukhjeet realised that the eagerness with which he said this was unwittingly revealing his overwhelming desire to cancel the entire plan and just continue with his life as was. He compensated by volunteering the answer to his own question. *'I guess they can always plant false evidence.'*

'Exactly,' his mother responded. *'Remember that boy from the village just here?'* She pointed in the direction of the kitchen. *'The police planted, what do they call it, that powder, oh, RDX powder. They planted RDX powder in his car*

and then arrested him. All because his father had a civil court case registered against a politician. And just think, that boy had a clean record. You now have this suspected sedition on yours, even if you have been released without charge. And let's not forget your uncle was a "dangerous militant" who was apparently "killed during a fierce firefight with police". Son, it isn't safe for you here. You are everything to me, I couldn't bear to lose you.'

Sukhjeet could see deep wrinkles entrenched across his mother's forehead. Her eyes were dark and puffy. Even the pupils themselves appeared to be a different, less vibrant shade to normal. She clearly hadn't slept restfully since this entire affair had erupted nearly a week prior. If he did manage to convince his parents that he should stay and even if the police did leave him alone, it was clear that they both would forever be on tenterhooks. Every time he was out later than planned, his mother would be lying awake in bed panicking. Every time his father opened the newspaper and read the headline about some youth being arrested, his blood pressure would rocket. And at that moment he knew that he needed to go, if not for his own safety then certainly for his parents' wellbeing. Not only that, he owed it to them to make his departure the following day as painless as possible. And so that is what he would do.

Digging deep, Sukhjeet invoked his inner comedian and actor, took his glass of milk and walked over towards his mother, falling theatrically onto the sofa next to her. 'Mom, if you wanted an excuse to go and visit England one day and see the Queen's palace, you should have just said so, no need for all this drama.'

Despite her despondency, his mother couldn't help but smile, albeit only briefly. And for that smile,

Sukhjeet reflected, he was prepared to sacrifice anything. She playfully patted his uninjured cheek, *'my dear son, always has some silly upside-down back-to-front take on everything!'*

But for the sporadic slurping of hot milk, a long period of introspective silence then ensued, nobody wanting to further sour the already sombre mood by bringing up their deep and justifiable concerns for what the future might hold. Even when they did eventually start chatting again, though the conversation flowed seemingly unendingly, they talked only trivia, just appreciative of the opportunity to spend this precious time together.

They mused about how Sukhjeet should be careful about all those flirty English girls falling in love with him and to be sure to look for a nice Punjabi girl to marry. The irony was that he had never formally discussed Anita with them; the perfect Punjabi girl he had already found but with whom he could no longer map out any possible future.

They talked politics, like never before. About injustices and how India had descended into corruption fuelled decay since the day the British left. About how Sikhs, as a minority group, had suffered under successive Hindu populist vote seeking governments. But also, about how Sikhs were prepared to savage fellow Sikhs for just a few Rupees and to what depths the community had descended in its lack of solidarity. About the drugs epidemic sweeping across Punjab; narcotics allowed to flow freely from Afghanistan and Pakistan into Punjab as all the border officials were in the pockets of the drug lords. The fact that the government had turned a blind eye to his. What better way to silence a politically awakened community like the Sikhs but to hook its youth onto drugs?

But talk about the future remained largely off limits. Except that everything would turn out OK. They just needed to be stoic through the initial hardships. The question of how Sukhjeet would gain longer term legitimacy to live in the UK was left to God to answer. He would find a way so they all just needed to have faith.

After what seemed like minutes but was actually many hours, daylight started to creep into the room from around the edges of the curtains that had been uncharacteristically drawn shut these past few nights. The significance was clear but it fell to Sukhjeet's father to prompt the others into ending what was possibly their last ever night sat together as one family. *'Sukhjeet, it is time for my morning prayers. And you should all get a little sleep.'*

'Daddy ji. I am sorry.'

'Son, what....'

Sukhjeet stood up, adding further weight to his words. *'I am sorry for putting you both in this situation. I didn't mean to....'* He couldn't find the words to articulate his apology clearly but he didn't need to. His father stopped him mid-sentence, gesturing 'shush' by putting his index fingers against his own lips. He got up and walked over to his son, placing both hands on his shoulders.

'Son. You haven't done anything wrong. You did what you thought was right and indeed was objectively right. You were raising a voice for justice and protesting the wrongs that have been meted out to poor innocent folk. That is our duty as Sikhs. There is nothing to apologise for. Never have even a morsel of regret for what you did. I am proud I raised a son like you. And going forward, never be scared. Face every chal-

lenge head on and stay true to your principles, just like our forefathers did before us. The rest is in Vaheguru's hands; He will keep you safe. Never lose your faith in Him.'

Sukhjeet felt his eyes welling up and his jaw quivered. Desperate not to let his father witness him crying, he leant forward to hug him and took a consciously deep breath to try and quell the gushing emotions building up inside. The duo soon felt a third pair of arms engulf them and all three stood perfectly still, savouring the moment but all consciously withholding their tears for fear of upsetting the others.

It was mid-morning when Sukhjeet rang Anita. They had spoken a few times on the phone over the past few days and after she had sworn to secrecy on his life, he had told her that he would be leaving the country. He had softened the blow by disingenuously suggesting that it may be a temporary measure. However, he felt he owed her the truth and, in this conversation today, he revealed the fact that it would, in fact, be permanent.

'So that's it then. It's all over? Everything we had together? All our dreams? Don't do this Sukhi,' came the sobbing voice over the phone.

Sukhjeet surprised himself with his resoluteness. He had already overcome the toughest obstacle of facing up to the reality of abandoning his parents and leaving them all alone in the world. With Anita, he felt he was actually doing her a favour. He was sacrificing his love and setting her free, sparing her painful years ahead futilely anticipating his return. She would find someone else with whom she could build a life, soon enough. 'Anita, what can we do? We have no choice.'

'I can come to England. I can enrol on a college course.

We can be together. There is always a choice.'

'And who will support us? I don't even know if I will be able to work or what I will be doing. I will be a "soldier", Anita, a "freshie", an "illegal immigrant", whatever you want to call it, probably doing manual labour somewhere if I am lucky.'

'Let me come and see you before you go at least. Please! I will find a way to get to you from Delhi in the next few days. I will work something out.'

'There is no time, Anita. I leave India today. Anyhow, I can't allow myself to put you through any more pain than I already have.' His comments were met with silence. *'Anita, I love you from the bottom of my heart. And I will never be able to love anyone in this way again. That is precisely why I am telling you that you mustn't wait for me. I may never be able to return. I won't even be able to ring you or my parents, the very people I love most. The police are likely to tap any phones they know I might try to call. This is my personal misfortune Anita. I am paying for whatever misdeeds I committed in a previous life. I cannot drag you down with me.'*

And with that phone-call, one of the happiest chapters of his entire life was permanently closed.

That evening, as the taxi pulled away from his village and he embarked on the ten-hour journey to New Delhi international airport, Sukhjeet reflected on his last moments at home. What sort of destiny was this? His parents couldn't make any fuss about their only son leaving home, potentially forever. He couldn't say goodbye to his friends. He had been unable to see Anita one last time. And now he wouldn't even be able to speak to his loved ones by phone for at least two years and then after that he would just be chancing it, assuming it was safe to ring without any way to confirm it. His parents hadn't even been able to accompany their only son to the taxi to wish him well, for fear of attracting undue neighbours' attention. Instead, they had said their final farewells stood just inside the front door. Nobody had cried. His parents received their strength from their faith. He had always known this but it had become crystal clear to him when they all visited the small village gurdwara earlier. Both his parents emerged with spirits uplifted, as if somehow God Himself had spoken to them directly to say everything would be OK. Sukhjeet asked for only thing when they had all bowed their heads in obeisance in front of the Guru Granth Sahib; an explanation. Why had this happened to him and his family? What had he done to deserve this?

His own strength came from the feeling of injustice, deep in his gut. He would survive, he would make a success of his life, and he would be back together with his parents. Maybe not this year or the next, but he would do it. Any other outcome would mean that tyranny had prevailed and his family had lost. He simply would not allow that to be how his life panned out. He stopped looking back out the taxi's rear window and snapped his neck around to face forwards, reflecting intently on his father's advice. Yes, he would be strong. Yes, he would face all the difficulties head on. And, yes, he wouldn't let any obstacles stand in his path. He still felt deeply sad but sensed a definite wave of self-assurance pass through his body. Yet unbeknown to him, it was this inner confidence and willpower that would keep him alive over the arduous months coming up ahead.

9B. Wolverhampton, England: December 2016

D ark clouds hung low in the sky, blocking out virtually all the mid-afternoon sunlight and giving an even gloomier backdrop to the absolutely desolate streets. Not that it really mattered to most people, for everyone was at home, busy gluttonously celebrating Christmas day with their families. And as for Sukhjeet, practically nothing could have dampened his mood today. Palpably exited, he was speed-walking his way to Zainab's apartment, where they would be sharing their first Christmas together.

Despite having supposedly had his apology unequivocally accepted when they met at college a few days after the 'incident' on the way home from Pizza Express, Sukhjeet had been treading carefully around Zainab during their meetings since, tactfully avoiding any potentially sensitive topics. This invisible and seemingly fluid line of political correctness was difficult for him to fully grasp. He was more accustomed to the Indian way, blurting out exactly what he thought without too much consideration for the recipient's feelings. However, he had been in the UK for over eighteen months now so not having a better grasp of how of conversations were conducted here was not acceptable, he told himself. On the positive side, the 'incident' had forced him to take out some time to consciously ruminate this and when he did, the reasons behind his slow absorption of British traits and values were readily identifiable. He had to face up to it; he really only existed on the margins of society. Hence, it was no surprise he was failing to unravel the nuances of the culture. Working purely with Eastern European builders, only socialising with his Punjabi immigrant housemates, not taking part in any activities or sport, complete detachment from what was happening in the country at large. He needed to change his ways and vowed to do so. Whether he liked it or not, and clearly not out of choice, he was nevertheless in the UK, without any intention to leave of his own volition. So, it was high time he started taking a longer-term view. Squirrelling away all his cash and living a closeted life in the manner he had been, wasn't sensible. Frugality was fine but there was clearly a need to invest something into his future here. He had always been put-off by the idea of nurturing his British life too much due to the constant threat of deportation he lived under. But he was still here eighteen months on and, at some point, he had to move forward under the assumption that he would be staying, rather than the counter-productive converse, of living in constant limbo under the assumption that he wouldn't. He had to stop expecting the Border Police to kick down his front door at any time, or humiliatingly man-handle him off a building site one day. He laid out some simple, logical steps he could take, quite impressed with himself when he had done so. Firstly, he swore to read more widely and had already started by taking advantage of the free newspapers provided in the town library, visiting it on Wednesdays after work, when it was open late. Eventually, he planned to also purchase a cheap e-tablet so he could access the news. Remarkable even to him when he actually thought about it, he had hardly accessed the internet at all since he arrived in the UK. He had gotten a sinking feeling in the pit of his stomach whenever he had considered heading to an internet café and logging on. How remarkably easy it would be to access an online Punjabi newspaper and catch up on goings-on back home? But the prospect of uncovering bad news from home frightened him. Equally, he feared what else he might find online. Perhaps feeling he would be unable to bear it if social media exposed to him how successfully his family and friends had managed to move on with their own lives despite his absence. Evidently, he needed to overcome all these unconstructive emotions but decided to postpone accessing the internet until after he had made the much awaited first telephone call to his parents. After all, the promised two years point since his departure from India was finally coming up, in only two months' time.

So, in this way, what had started as confused, rambling thoughts, had now all been formulated into a coherent set of 'new year's resolutions,' a term he had only heard a week prior. He looked forward to telling Zainab all about them.

Zainab lived in one of the newer developments just outside the city centre. These had been built around ten years prior. Luxury two- and three-bedroom apartments in a canal-side development, to cater for the throngs of professionals supposedly wanting to live somewhere more economical than but within easy reach of Birmingham, or perhaps attracted to Wolverhampton itself for its own expanding employment market and cultural scene. However, the town had not been immune to ripple effects of the global financial crisis. Industry investors had pulled their funding and the much-hyped job opportunities never materialised. As a result, the profile of residents within the development was clearly not what had been intended. However, though undeniably starting to enter early stages of disrepair, with uncleaned graffiti on walls and rubbish sheds overflowing with bin bags, it was still far nicer than Sukhjeet's street.

So, dressed in yet more new clothes and doused in aftershave, he finally arrived. He had rehearsed his planned, initial sequence of actions many times. As soon as she opened the front door, he would lean in determinedly and confidently for a kiss. Unfortunately, he had not accounted for the buzzer he would have to ring in order to enter the main block. By the time he had been buzzed-in and had climbed up the stairs to her second-floor apartment, she was already waiting for him at her door. He lost his nerve a little and fumbled around handing over the bunch of flowers he had brought along and wishing her 'merry Christmas'. He then made what he felt was a commendable effort to get back on track, leaning forward for that kiss, but Zainab turned her head sufficiently that he missed her lips and caught her cheek, after which she put her arms around him and they hugged instead.

As he entered the apartment itself, for the first time, Sukhjeet was struck by how tidy and homely it had been kept by Zainab and her flatmate, who was back at her parental home in Leeds for Christmas. A vase with dried bamboo in one corner, a stylish red metal shade over the dining table, wooden floors, a pastel portrait of generic European countryside on the wall. It was obvious that there was nothing particularly expensive here but it was undeniably very tastefully put together. He contrasted it to his own house with its fraying, musty carpets, the milk crate next to the sofa as an extra seat, torn linoleum flooring in the kitchen, plastic buckets in the bath-tub. He could never invite Zainab to his house, that much was clear.

As promised, Zainab had prepared a Palestinian food feast. It wasn't in any way a traditional Christmas lunch but that particular concept didn't really mean anything to either of them anyway. Zainab excitedly talked Sukhjeet through the meal, reciprocating the degree of enthusiasm he had exhibited about his own native dishes during their first dinner together at the curry restaurant. Astonishing for both of them, that had been only two months prior. Now look at them, sharing Christmas together. 'So, these triangular ones are fatayer sabanekh. Bit like your Punjabi samosas, but not so spicy. And this is a very traditional soup, made with lentils, called shorbet adas.'

'Shorbet, like "sharbat" in Punjab, the same word' Sukhjeet commented, as he slurped up a hot mouthful. It was delicious, a milder version of Indian lentil dhal but with a much stronger lemony zest that tickled the back of the throat. He enthusiastically refilled his spoon. 'It's very, very tasty. Wow. I am impressed!'

'Thanks,' said Zainab, smiling, 'have some sabanekh too.' She held up the foil-lined oven tray and Sukhjeet took three. 'Wow, hungry eh?'

'You said come hungry, so now you best not try to bloody stop me!'

Zainab chuckled, dipping into her own shorbet. 'Don't worry, there are plenty more dishes to come.' She then poured out some sparkling apple juice for them both, from a fancy bottle that popped like champagne when she removed the cork. Zainab held up the glass in front of her, prompting Sukhjeet to stop eating momentarily and do the same. Energetic bubbles shot up, right out the top of the glass, before falling back into the fizzing golden liquid, seemingly also rejoicing in the festive excitement. 'Cheers! Merry Christmas, Sukhi.'

'Cheers! Merry Christmas, Zainab.' And then, surprising even himself with his spontaneity, he followed up with, 'thanks for coming into my life. I am grateful for that every day.' They looked into each other's eyes, silently. As always, it didn't feel staged or awkward. Sukhjeet wasn't nervous or on edge. He had confidently and honestly expressed an emotion from the bottom of his heart; one that he hadn't even known he felt. But it was clear to him now. He was grateful. Zainab was undoubtedly the singular best thing that had happened to him since he left Punjab. She had been the one who had made the effort to befriend him, and that deserved his gratitude.

Eventually, visible even under the dim ambient lighting in the room, Zainab's cheeks flushed a little and she looked down, unnecessarily stirring her shorbet with her soup spoon. 'Thank you,' she said, consciously forcing herself to overcome her sudden coyness and look back up. 'That's a really sweet thing to say. It means a lot.'

The rest of the meal also did not disappoint. Zainab's maqloubeh, though very filling, was incredibly moreish. Sukhjeet relished the fragrant brown rice, fluffy in a way only fresh home-cooked rice can be. The dish was absolutely bursting with flavour, distinct to the Indian food he was accustomed to but not entirely unfamiliar. He was able to taste the cardamom, cinnamon and hints of spice and their powerful aromas filled his senses with delight, compelling him to have three helpings.

Having gorged beyond all necessity, Sukhjeet was now collapsed on the nearby sofa to recuperate, his only half-genuine offer to help clear the dishes thankfully having been politely rejected. And then, as Zainab busily cleared the dishes from the table and Sukhjeet could just sense himself dosing off, she unexpectedly broke into song. Mesmerising acapella, Arabic lyrics filled the room, disturbed sporadically by the clanging of cutlery and crockery as it was methodically cleared up. Zainab continued going about her business, seemingly oblivious to the impact her angelic voice was having on Sukhjeet. However, once she finished hand-washing those last few bulky items that wouldn't fit in the dishwasher, she turned to face Sukhjeet, acknowledging his presence with a smile and a wink as she continued to sing. Her confidence was well deserved; she held pitch-perfect tone. Sukhjeet didn't actually understand a word of the lyrics, yet somehow, he felt the song resonate deep inside him and it drew him out of his slumber, compelling him to stand up and walk over towards her, awestruck.

He put his arms around her, in a tender embrace and felt no resistance. In fact, she reciprocated, squeezing him tightly and lowering her voice so that her singing became melodious whispers in his ears, as she nested her cheek on his muscular shoulders. Sukhjeet didn't want her to stop her singing, but he needed to kiss her, right there and then. He nudged her back a little and they looked at each other intently, nothing else in the world mattering to either of them. Despite the stark silence in the room when Zainab did abruptly stop singing, there was no unease. Their heads moved together in seemingly rehearsed unison and two pairs of lips fused together as if they had finally found their true, pre-ordained purpose in life. He relished the texture of her soft lips, every crease, every dimple, every curve. He initially dared not open his eyes in case this was a dream, but when he did momentarily do so, he was greeted by a beautiful sight; Zainab's alluringly flushed face bonded with his, long eyelashes tickling his cheek as she reached up to run her hands through his hair. Splashes of coloured illumination danced across her face. Even the Christmas lights hung around her window were partaking in their magical moment. Just as their tongues almost touched, Zainab pulled back. Sliding her hands down from his hair, across his face and then eventually parting from him at his shoulders, she walked backwards to the window. Drawing the curtains closed she blocked out all the light from the streetlamps and festive lights, leaving them only with the gentle flickering of the candle on the table. She picked up her mobile phone and within seconds the room was filled with mellow Arabic beats. But the real surprise was yet to come. With sensual poise, she walked back towards Sukhjeet, keeping her eyes locked with his. Reaching up, she untied her hijab, placing it on the back of a chair whilst shaking her hair out. Magnificent, long, caramel locks, beautifully curly, fell loose to below her shoulders. She took the final steps towards him but he met her half way, magnetically drawn towards her. 'Where were we?' she said softly, placing her arms delicately back around his neck.

SECTION 10: LIFE'S SURPRISES

'Hope is important because it can make the present moment less difficult to bear. If we believe that tomorrow will be better, we can bear a hardship today.' Thich Nhat Hanh.

10A. Moscow, Russia: Feb 2015

Sukhjeet walked out of Sheremetyevo International Airport, trailing diligently fifteen metres behind the intimidatingly burly, heavily tattooed, skinhead man in the leather jacket, exactly as instructed by him in broken English only moments prior. As per the plan clearly explained to Sukhjeet by the agent, Shivjot Kumar, back in Punjab, the two men had rendezvoused at the ATM machine next to the row of bustling currency exchange kiosks in the arrival hall, where they had conversed subtly under their breath and even that only for a few seconds. Sukhjeet kept his head down as he walked, his chin buried in his jacket collar to protect himself against the biting cold. But he peered up frequently, to ensure he didn't lose track of his courier but also to gape in bewilderment at the mounds of hardened snow piled up at the edges of the pavement. Snow was not how he had imagined it. He expected it to be bright white, light and fluffy, like the ski-slopes of Switzerland he had seen featured in so many Bollywood movies. Yet here was the real thing, disappointingly tainted in mud, grit and diesel fumes. Perhaps this was what growing up was all about. A depressing realignment of reality versus the naive expectations of youth. Just look at his own life, already turning out poles apart from his dreams.

Moscow in February is an unforgiving place. Sukhjeet's hands were numb with cold despite being tucked into his pockets and the freezing gale seemed to tear right the way through him. However, he still lost all track of time during the walk. Sensory overload from the bustling crowds of Caucasian faces, many donning ushankas – the traditional Russian furry hat, the multitude of indecipherable Cyrillic signs and dense but highly ordered traffic flow made the half hour walk seem like only a few minutes. Eventually, they arrived in a muddy, make-shift car park backing onto an industrial estate serving the airport. Sukhjeet was led to an aging, red van which had another similarly thuggish looking Russian fast asleep in the driver's seat. Whilst being ushered into the back, the first thing that hit him was the overwhelming stench of human body odour. Next, following quite quickly, came fear. But with few options,

Sukhjeet tried to avoid dwelling on his sense of dread cum panic and manoeuvred warily onto the double mattress that was laid out on the van's floor, perching himself on the corner closest to the door. He had noticed the two men sat on the far side of the mattress but was unable to inspect them more thoroughly as he had been busy looking around to see if there were fold-down seats to sit on, which there weren't. The door slammed shut and they were plunged into near total darkness, before the van aggressively pulled away, the acceleration shunting Sukhjeet painfully against the wheel arch.

From soon after they started moving, Sukhjeet could hear the men murmuring to each other and even with the minimal light, he could make out that they were looking in his direction as they did so. It was difficult to identify the language; Persian or Arabic was Sukhjeet's guess. Without obviously looking down, Sukhjeet subtly felt around for his rucksack with his feet and once he located it, slipped his leg through the straps, physically attaching himself to it. 'Where come?' came a gruff voice from the man sitting furthest away and who seemed either to be wearing a scarf or had a long beard.

'Punjab,' replied Sukhjeet, following up quickly with, 'in India.' Sukhjeet's answer sparked a lively discussion amongst the two men and he could feel his heart beating faster, but he took the plunge. 'And where are you from?' he queried.

This time it was the closer seated man that spoke. 'Namaste! My name Iqbal. My friend Sajed. We Afghan.' And then, unexpectedly, he broke into broken but understandable Hindi. *'What is your name'?*

'Oh. Errm, my name is Sukhjeet.' Sukhjeet started extending an arm to shake their hand but quickly realised

they were sat way too far away. So, he just ended up gesticulating nervously in a bizarre half-wave half-salute.

'We are from Ghazni. You heard of that?'

'Sorry, no I don't know where that is. When did your plane land here? Where you waiting a long time in the van for me?'

Iqbal clapped and then said something to Sajed whilst chuckling. Iqbal then explained the joke. 'We cannot afford to fly here. We came in a truck brother.' Great. So, they clearly saw Sukhjeet as a privileged rich kid being whisked off to the European Union by his parents. That is just what he needed.

The van turned a corner and the altered direction of the sunlight cast a little more light into the compartment. A few stray but bright beams now found their way through moth-holes in the thick, black curtain that was drawn across the small glass window built into the partition between them in the back and the driver and escort seated in the front. As a result, Sukhjeet was able to get a better picture of the men. Sajed did indeed have a long beard whereas Iqbal sported more of an overgrown stubble. Both were dressed in typical Western attire, albeit noticeably grubby. 'How long did it take to get here from your town?'

Sajed replied. His Hindi was even better than Iqbal's but he was clearly the less upbeat of the two. 'We have been transported like animals in the back of trucks for the past three weeks.'

There was venom in Sajed's voice and not knowing how to respond to that Sukhjeet thought it best to change subject quickly. 'How do you both have such good Hindi?'

This was definitely Iqbal's territory. 'Really, is it

good? Wah! Sajed, my Hindi is good. Maybe I can be the next Amitabh Bachan, dancing with all those beauties in wet saris.' He then started twirling his arms around in mock Indian dance moves that made Sukhjeet laugh out loud and even elicited a smile from Sajed, his bright, yellow teeth beaming into the dim light.

After about three hours of driving, the van pulled over. Before the door was opened for them, Sukhjeet distinctly heard keys being inserted into a padlock and some sort of metallic latch being undone. Sure enough, as they clambered out the back, knees stiff from the discomfort of the journey, Sukhjeet spotted the heavy-duty lock amateurishly welded onto the van door. They were parked in the far corner of a motorway service station, surrounded by trucks and the odd coach. The two Russians started to walk towards the main service area and Sukhjeet was pulled back from following them by Iqbal grabbing his arm. *'We don't go that way. You may have come by aeroplane and us by truck, Sukhjeet brother, but we are all the same "donkeys" now.'* The Afghans clearly knew the drill well. They jumped over a short fence and led Sukhjeet down a small bank towards some bushes where they relieved themselves. Upon returning back to the van, they climbed into the back and waited for the Russians, who appeared about half an hour later and flung them a plastic bag containing small water bottles, a loaf of dry bread and three lukewarm pasties filled with a bland, oily stew. As the men distributed the rations, Sukhjeet heard the metal latch sliding into place and the padlock clicking shut. Once again, they were on the move.

Sukhjeet began to lose track of time. His back was

starting to ache from the effects of the van's poor suspension and general strain of sitting contortedly, so he opted to copy the Afghans and lie down on the mattress. Put off initially by the dampness and odours, he had pulled up his rucksack to use as a pillow and also to put some distance between his nostrils and the mattress surface. It worked. He had now been awake for over a day and quickly fell into a deep slumber that lasted the rest of the journey.

As they clambered out the van, they were greeted by a blizzard. Sukhjeet impulsively hugged his rucksack to protect himself against the belting, horizontal sleet and all the men raced into a tall, grey, concrete, communist-era tower-block, led by the Russians. Red tape was criss-crossed across the two lifts, so they started ascending the stairs, the driver taking the lead with the escort bringing up the rear. They climbed up what felt like dozens of floors. Though each floor had a sign that depicted a number, these were in Cyrillic so indecipherable. However, Sukhjeet noted that the symbols had acquired two digits some time ago suggesting they were surely into the twenty or thirty something floors by now.

Stopping abruptly outside a bright green door, the Russian at the head of the group began to make a call on his mobile phone and Sukhjeet took the opportunity to catch his breath and look around. The corridor was utterly uninviting, with a concrete floor that was so cold Sukhjeet could feel it chilling his feet through the soles of his shoes. Tattered remnants of laminate flooring survived along the edges but it was otherwise bare. Small pools of water were dotted around, doubtless leaking from the tangle of pipework that was exposed in the ceiling. Large, black, patches of damp were littered across the walls, with the paintwork in a state of complete disrepair. Sukhjeet gravitated towards the window at the end of the corridor, desperate to investigate what he could see from such a high vantage point. He used the opportunity to again try and estimate how high up they were, reckoning about twenty-five floors. It looked like they were in a small town though in the distance, beyond acres of lush, green pine forest, Sukhjeet could see a sizeable urban conurbation, with plumes of industrial smoke billowing into the sky, forming thick pillars that looked like they were holding up the multitude of grey clouds.

'*Oi, sister-fucker!*' Sukhjeet turned around, very pleased to be hearing Punjabi, even though he was being sworn at.

'*Get back over here. You think you on a sight-seeing cruise or what?*' The first thing that struck Sukhjeet about the man that was shouting at him was his sheer size. He must have been at least six feet six inches tall, with a very stocky physique, and that wasn't just an illusion caused by the thick bomber jacket he was wearing. Clean-shaven apart from a neatly trimmed moustache, his fair skin, prominent nose and high-set cheeks certainly gave his face a Punjabi look.

Sukhjeet started walking back towards the other men, struggling to work out where the newcomer had appeared from. He must have descended from one of the higher floors. '*Sorry brother,*' Sukhjeet said, '*I was just...*'

'*Hey. I am not your sister-fucking brother. To you, I am Abdul Khan. Got it?*'

Sukhjeet nodded. Of course. How could he have not picked that up from his dialect? He was clearly Pakistani Punjabi.

Abdul fumbled with an enormous bunch of keys and eventually managed to gain access to the room, pushing the door wide open. The Afghans were the first to walk in. They seemed a lot less fazed by things than Sukhjeet. Perhaps they had just been in this situation many times before over the past weeks and simply knew what to expect. Sukhjeet hesitantly followed them into the dark hallway. The light switch had been pulled off the wall, leaving a bunch of exposed electrical wires protruding ominously outwards. Taking a wide berth around the hazard, he was soon safely in the living room. It was a large, open room, with a small stove in the far corner. Six grimy mattresses lay on the floor, with an assortment of stained blankets and pillows piled up high on one of them. There were sizeable windows but these were locked shut and the panes of glass had been coarsely painted over on the interior. Outside the door, Sukhjeet could hear Abdul speaking to the others in what was presumably Russian and a few moments later the three men appeared in the room. Abdul pulled a pack of cigarettes out from his pocket and lit one up, proceeding to stroll around the room offering them to each of the other men. The Russians and Afghans quickly took him up on the seemingly generous offer and then it was Sukhjeet's turn. He declined, trying hard not to make a disparaging facial expression. *'Go on. Have one.'* Abdul said.

'No thanks.' Sukhjeet replied, in English.

'Why?'

'I don't smoke.'

Abdul eyed him up and down curiously. At first, Sukhjeet thought it was the gauze across his face that was inviting interest. But he quickly realised Abdul was looking down towards his wrists, which were covered by his jacket sleeve, preventing Abdul from seeing his Karra. *You Sikh?'*

Sukhjeet nodded.

'OK, that's fine, "brother"' said Abdul, sarcastically, before blowing a large puff of smoke straight into Sukhjeet's face. Wisely, Sukhjeet managed to resist the almost impulsive urge to lunge at him, containing his annoyance at this flagrant insult. Abdul turned back towards the Afghans.

'You speak Hindi?' he quizzed.

'Yes sir.' Iqbal answered, enthusiastically.

'You are going to ring your parents from my phone and tell them to make the outstanding payment.'

'That is supposed to be paid only once we are in France. I have no idea where we are but we cannot be in France already. A deal is a deal.' Though he looked a nervous, the tone of Sajed's voice was assertive.

'When I want your answer, I will ask you the question. Until then, keep your mouth shut.' Abdul turned back to face Iqbal. *'So, here is my phone.'* He pulled out a state-of-the-art iPhone and unlocked the screen. *'What is the number to call them on?'*

Iqbal looked worried. *'Brother...'*

Abdul raised the volume of his voice when he replied. *'Hey! I am not your brother any more than I am that mother-fucking Indian's brother.'* He softened his tone again. *'So, let's no waste any more time. We will get you to France, but you need to ring your parents NOW and tell them to release the rest of the money.'*

'But...'

Suddenly and with lightning speed, Abdul grabbed Iqbal's head with one hand and took the lit cigarette out of his mouth with the other, stubbing it out on his neck, pushing it hard against him until it was extinguished. The sizzle of melting skin could be heard even above the piercing, squealing sound Iqbal made. Sajed took one step towards Iqbal but froze in his tracks as the two Russians also moved closer to the unfolding drama in response.

'Don't fuck around with me. I will beat you so hard your next generations will quiver from it. Want your face to look more fucked than that sister-fucking Indian over there? Huh?' Abdul glanced over at Sukhjeet, who was stood still, completely expressionless, stunned into a state of complete inaction. 'You two,' said Abdul, now pointing back and forth at the two Afghans with his one spare hand, having thrown the cigarette on the floor but still clutching onto Iqbal by his hair. 'You two mother-fuckers are going to ring your parents now and tell them to release the money. Then, you are going to wait quietly here a few days until we move you out of Ukraine and into Europe.'

The distinct reek of charred flesh hung in the air and they all nodded in unison, including Iqbal, who bobbed his head up and down as best he could. He was eventually released to tend to his festering wound, but only after both Afghans had made the calls home.

10B. Wolverhampton, England: Jan 2017

The therapeutic whirring of the portable fan heater was the only noise in the room, gently nudging Sukhjeet into a sleepy slumber, like his mother's lullabies had done during his infant days. His breathing deepened and the duvet covering his chest started to rise and fall as he began dozing off. This attracted Zainab's attention and she knew she needed to act quickly to ensure that their valuable time together was not lost to his siesta.

'Sukhi.'

'*Haan meri jaan.*' He impulsively replied in Punjabi before abruptly correcting himself and fully awakening in the process. 'Err...why the hell am I talking in Punjab? Stupid. Sorry, yes, what is it?'

'What does that mean?'

'What?'

'*Haan meri jaan.*' Though not entirely perfect, Zainab was able to repeat the Punjabi phrase with an impressive degree of accuracy and apt intonation.

Sukhjeet smiled. 'It is a way of replying to someone you care for very much. "Haan" means "yes", "meri" means "my", and "jaan" means "life"…or "sweetheart" in this context. Anyway, what's up?'

Zainab remained focused on her newfound line of enquiry. 'Is that what you used to call Anita, "meri jaan"?'

Silence ensued as Sukhjeet pondered how little he had actually thought about Anita these past few months. It was almost like, despite all the romantic ideals, his heart was no more sophisticated than a bucket. Feelings for Anita had to be drained out to make room for loving Zainab. It saddened him to think that life was actually so transactional. He has been so convinced that Anita was 'the one', irreplaceable to the point that Sukhjeet pledged to remain single all his life rather than love or marry anyone else. In fact, he had proclaimed this very fact to her dramatically, on many occasions. Yet, here he was, lying in bed next to Zainab. So quickly reconciled to the reality of his new life. So quick to drop the old and embrace the new. Sad, really. Or was it? Perhaps the willingness and ability to adapt so readily was just human instinct, a necessity for survival, something to be lauded? He reflected that what he really wondered most, on those occasions when Anita did enter his thoughts, was whether she too had moved on. He couldn't imagine her with anyone else but of course she needed to build her own life. Anyway, by now, even in the unlikely event she had been too traumatised to find new love herself, she would have graduated from university and her parents would be searching for eligible suitors. But there was an uneasy niggle, deep in the darkest corners of his soul where he dared not hunt too hard, that hoped she was still longing for him. Why? Perhaps, he thought, if at least one of them held on dearly to the memories of their romance it somehow meant it had been real. Otherwise, hadn't everything about their experience together just vanished, destroyed by circumstance? That really would be too sad to accept willingly.

'Do you still think about her?' Zainab's tone was entirely matter of fact. If there was any underlying emotion or expectation as to what his answer would be, she hid it very well.

'Not since I met you.'

'You don't have to say what you think I want to hear, Sukhi.'

'I am telling the truth. I used to think about her a lot. But, since I met you, I hardly think about her at all. I feel bad about that. I thought I loved her, but maybe I didn't know what love is until now.'

Zainab turned towards him and pulled her arm out from under the duvet and began stroking his cheek. 'I am sure you did love her.'

'I love only you now Zainab, that's all that matters.'

'And I love you, Mister Sukhjeet Singh, particularly your innocence.' Not wanting to make any sudden moves that might interrupt the moment, she opted against leaning over to kiss him and instead touched her lips with her index finger and then planted it on his lips. She followed with a question, her tone giving away its rhetorical nature. 'So, you think you can only love one person in your life?'

'Don't you?'

'No. I don't.'

Sukhi widened his eyes and opened his mouth in mock horror. This was purely to come across as comfortable with whatever liberal idea Zainab was about to present, though in actual fact, he was a little perturbed and keen to understand more deeply precisely what principle she was espousing here.

She went on to explain, lowering her voice even further, now down to barely a whisper, toying with his sideburn hairs as she spoke. 'I think we are on this planet to love, to love lots of people, but you will not be able to love two people in the same way. Even your parents, you may love them equally but the love will be different for your mum and dad. Right?'

The question resurrected a barrage of childhood memories in Sukhjeet's mind. Going crying to his mother every time he suffered a scrape, confident he would receive unadulterated sympathy whereas his father would berate him for climbing trees or cycling off-road in the first place. Just the slightest turning up of his nose at a dish and how his mother would happily start preparing a new meal for him from scratch, without even the slightest reluctance. But his father had his own very special place in his heart. Those long days spent repairing and then test-driving the tractor. Going to pick up their brand-new combine harvester from the showroom and his father allowing Sukhjeet to drive as they paraded it through the village. His father buying him a Bullet motorcycle when he won his scholarship at the prestigious Guru Nanak Dev University Amritsar, despite his mother's protestations about the safety implications. He missed them both so much. He took some solace in the fact that very soon two years would be up and he could at least ring them without breaking his no-contact vow. 'Yes, of course you love your parents the same amount but in different ways. But love between a man and woman is....'

Zainab cut him short. 'It's the same for romantic

love. I think love is a gift from God and as such it has no limits, it's infinite. We can love again and again. But everything about our passion and feelings for a future or past lover will be completely different to those that we have for the person with whom we are with today.'

'What if I don't want anyone else in the future?' Sukhjeet didn't really think through what response to his question he wanted from Zainab. It just seemed like the right thing to ask.

'Oh Sukhi.' He didn't appreciate the infantilising tone and suddenly her stroking his hair started to annoy him a little. 'There is so much in this world we cannot control. I have seen so many hopes and desires smashed. Individuals' hopes, families' hopes, even hopes and aspirations of entire nations, all turned to dust, by deceit, greed, selfishness or simply bad luck. So, to avoid a lifetime of disappointments, I aim to completely lose myself in every moment rather than worry too much about what will happen when it ends. Enjoy and savour that instant, because that is something that nobody can ever take away from you.'

Sukhjeet was perplexed. He couldn't help but agree with the ideas presented, but they seemed to somehow clash with the culturally peddled absolute truths that he was more accustomed to since childhood. Romantic love is reserved for only one individual, for the entire duration of your existence on this planet; life is not about savouring moments but a relentless and likely painful struggle towards the betterment of your family and your community; rewards for your endeavours would be received in an after-life. On balance, he certainly preferred Zainab's take on it.

As he lay contemplating, Zainab continued to

stroke his hair, causing the duvet to slip down her arm a little. Sukhjeet's attention instantly gravitated towards her ample, enticingly pert breast, which was starting to protrude from her peach, silk camisole top. Almost instantly, his heartrate began to quicken and animalistic passions started to well up inside, taking control of his actions. Turning to prop himself onto his elbow, he faced towards her, firmly grabbed her hand, which was still gently caressing his hair, and lifted it above her head, pinning it down against the pillow. She playfully struggled a little at first, going along with the game, but quickly realised she was entirely powerless against his hot-blooded strength. He readjusted his weight onto his other elbow, whilst keeping her arm immobilised, and grabbed her free hand, bringing it up to join the other prisoner, his one hand easily capable of encompassing and restraining both her dainty wrists. Completely taken aback by Sukhjeet's adept manoeuvring, Zainab suddenly felt his now spare hand making his way up her top, roughly yanking it aside in a way that was not characteristic of their previous lovemaking. Within seconds, she was exposed from the waist up to her neck, her camisole wrapped roughly around her upper chest.

'Sukhi!' she exclaimed. Calling out his name was intended as firm admonishment but the ever so slight quivering of her voice gave away her faltering. She persisted with increasingly feeble attempts to wriggle free but her own excitement was now starting to be laid bare by the stiffness of her pink nipples, that protruded out, longing for attention. Sukhjeet kneaded one with his fingers and Zainab closed her eyes, rolling her head back and rapturously digging it into the pillow in ecstasy. She then felt his hair tickle her upper chest as he took the other nipple into his mouth. Flooded with warm sensations flowing up and down her entire her body, she began moaning under her breath; music to Sukhjeet's ears. He released the grip on her hands but she didn't move them. She was sprawled out on the bed, being ravaged by her lover and at that moment she wanted nothing else. His hand wandered from her breast and moved down her smooth stomach. She hadn't realised how wet she was until he roughly moved her knickers aside and began stroking her. Hot, wet passion was pouring out, inviting him inside. Sukhjeet pulled himself upright sufficiently to pull off his boxers and in seconds she felt him enter her. They groaned in unison, each time he thrust into her. Pushing what remained of the duvet aside, she wrapped her legs around him, pulling him tight against her. Tongues collided, teeth nuzzled rampantly on lips and the mutual moaning intensified as they reached their explosive crescendo.

With her head on his chest, Zainab lay perfectly still, all her senses reflecting blissfully on the magic they had created together just moments prior. She could feel tiny beads of sweat from Sukhjeet's chest hairs against her cheek. She could hear his heart still pounding. The aroma of his aftershave was still alive in her nostrils. Unbeknown to Sukhjeet, she smiled widely. 'Sukhi,' she whispered.

'Yes.' He sounded half asleep again.

'That's exactly what I mean about losing yourself in the moment. I will certainly savour that memory for a long time. And judging from the noises you were making, I assume you will too?'

'Sure,' said Sukhjeet. But there won't be any need

to savour if we can just repeat whenever we want.'

Zainab started giggling and as well as hear Sukhjeet chuckling in response, she could actually feel the laughter deep in his belly too. Zainab waited until the merriment had died down a little. 'Well, at least we took advantage of my flatmate being away for the past few weeks. She comes back in a few days so we will need to find somewhere else to "lose ourselves in the moment". You sure we can't meet at your place?'

'My place is not a palace fit for a queen like you, Zainab.'

'Awww. That's so sweet, Sukhi. So, what will we do?' It was a question that had genuinely been perplexing them both these last few days but they hadn't talked openly about it. However, Sukhjeet had a plan. He had independently run through the finances and all the other numerous logistical and tedious, administrative implications and had concluded his proposal was worth peddling. He was purely waiting for the right timing and that moment had now clearly arrived.

So, after a short silence wondering how to broach it, Sukhjeet spoke. 'When does your joint tenancy contract with your friend expire?' Zainab looked baffled. 'As in, when could you move out of this apartment and into a different one, with someone else?'

SECTION 11: SURVIVAL INSTINCT

'There are no strangers here. Only friends you haven't met yet.' William Butler Yeats.

11A. Uzhanskyi National Park, Ukraine - Slovakia border: Mar 2015

'**G**ood luck mother-fuckers.' It was the first time Abdul had been seen to smile. Sukhjeet, on the other hand, was at his most nervous. The plan seemed to be littered with potential pitfalls. The three *'donkeys'* were to walk across a remote, supposedly un-patrolled stretch of the border, cross a river, regroup on the other side, ring a number saved onto a phone that had been provided, and then wait for a pick up. So much could go wrong. However, there was little choice in the matter. Abdul had been in no mood to discuss the contractual obligations associated with Sukhjeet's 'deluxe package', which had explicitly included the provision of an escort during every part of the journey. Meanwhile, Iqbal's still festering neck wound served effectively as a warning against more forceful protestation.

So, the trio set off into the dark, freezing night. Initially, moonlight provided sufficient illumination but soon they were descending towards the river bed. where thicker tree canopy cover blocked it out, slowing their advance considerably. The cold started to numb Sukhjeet's hands, the skin already cracking heavily from cumulative exposure over the past weeks to a degree of cold he just wasn't accustomed to. He had pulled down his jacket sleeves to cover them as best he could but he daren't put his hands away into his pockets as they were critical for breaking his fall when he slipped or stumbled, which was every few minutes. However, he kept his spirits up by considering the alternative. Yes, the ground may be cold and rock hard, hence undeniably painful when you fell on it. But surely it would be way worse in summer, when this whole floodplain would almost certainly transform into an insect infested, quicksand swamp.

Agitated by their walk, the latter part of which was in pitch darkness, and having been too wary of border guards to use the flashlight on the antiquated mobile phone they had been given, they eventually reached the river, which was starting to swell as snow gradually began melting in upstream highlands. *'Who wants to lead?'* Sukhjeet whispered. Silence ensued as everyone nervously surveyed the torrents of freezing water rushing past. *'At least one person should wait on the riverbank here until the others are safely across, so that we always have someone on land to raise the alarm if anyone gets injured or swept away.'* All three pondered the undeniably sensible suggestion for a moment but realised that it could cast them into a thorny moral dilemma. Would they really give-up all their dreams and aspirations and raise an alarm, assuring their own arrest and deportation by doing so, in order to help someone they had only met a few weeks ago, even if that person was in life-threatening distress? Sukhjeet soon piped up again, a subliminal ploy to distract himself from having to answer that soul-searching question. *'I think I can see some rocks we could use to step on. Shall I go first and try to find a route through?'*

'No. We will go first,' said Sajed, speaking on behalf of Iqbal too. *'We are Pashtuns; we are not frightened of anything.'* However, the slight trembling of his voice suggested otherwise. He was certainly frightened of something; the question was what. More so than the onerous river crossing, was it fear of getting stranded on this side all alone, Sukhjeet pondered? The Afghans whispered to each other in Pashto and then starting making their way across the river, trying to navigate via the rocks but quickly ending up just wading through the waist deep water, the rocks having proven to be too slippery to walk on.

The pair were about two-thirds of the way across when powerful car headlamps shone in the general direction of their position, from atop the ridge, about a kilometre away. There was no way a vehicle could ever traverse the intervening terrain and having just completed the journey, Sukhjeet also knew it would take at least fifteen minutes before any guards could reach them from that distance by foot. The Afghans were now into safer shallows on the far side, so Sukhjeet tightened his rucksack straps and also started to work his way through the river. Don't rush, don't rush, watch your step Sukhjeet, stay calm, he repeatedly told himself. The mantra was working and he kept his composure, diligently lodging one foot tightly under one of the many heavy rocks on the river bed, before taking a step with the other, ensuring he wouldn't get swept away with the current. However, his steady advance was interrupted by the unmistakable sound of a dog barking. He stopped his advance and twisted around, ignoring pleas from the Afghans for him to keep moving. Multiple flashlight beams could be seen criss-crossing each other in the distance, as the guards descended down the valley slopes. However, more pressingly, the barking was getting ever louder. Suddenly, out of the darkness of the forest and into the moonlight, a dog appeared, moving so fast that Sukhjeet didn't even have time to turn his body around fully before the beast was airborne, lunging straight at him from the riverbank, baring its menacing teeth.

Sukhjeet felt none of the much-fabled urge to fight nor a compulsion to take flight. Just a lightening-speed barrage of seemingly uncoordinated thoughts raced through his brain. Flashbacks of his parents, in their younger days, the way they had looked when he was a child. A disturbing image of his Cha-cha Ji's mutilated corpse outside the family home, as described by his father. Memories of scoring that celebrated goal in the final of the Punjab Universities Football Championships that ultimately secured a proud victory for his team. A fictional Anita at his bedside table, nursing him to health as he lay recovering following his police incarceration. Perhaps most bizarre, was the lingering realisation that his torn cheek had only just started to heal properly, the stiches having largely dissolved and his beard growth now sufficient to remove the gauze without leaving too unpalatable a scar visible. And now this ferocious dog would no doubt be mauling his face, undoing all the healing. If his parents were going to get a photograph of their dead son in the post, for their sake he didn't want to look violently assaulted. He started to bring his hands up to protect his face, but didn't have enough time for them to reach it.

The German Shepherd, kitted out in a black protective vest that made it look yet even more fearsome, landed squarely on Sukhjeet's chest, toppling him backwards into the water. They fell dramatically, smashing against a rock, the dog on top of Sukhjeet, sticking onto him like a limpet. The impact knocked the wind right out of his lungs and it was a few seconds before Sukhjeet got his bearings again. The rucksack had saved him from what could undoubtedly have been a serious back injury. However, during the fall, despite the initial shock, fear and general commotion, he did distinctly feel something snap in his knee. As he had collapsed backwards, his foot had remained awkwardly lodged under the rock, pointing outwards, where he had placed it for stability. What took longer to hit him was the associated, excruciating pain. For now, fuelled by adrenalin, he continued to thrash around, futilely wrestling with the dog but to no avail. The fifty-kilogram animal had him pinned up against the rock. It barked as loudly as it could, with a distinct and unmistakeably aggressive growling every time Sukhjeet tried to manoeuvre. Feeling entirely helpless, he soon resigned himself to the fact that its handlers would be upon him in minutes. It was game over. In fact, his primary struggle quickly became to just keep breathing. He was involuntarily swallowing significant quantities of water, his face barely above the river's surface, the dog simply not permitting him to sit any more upright.

Primarily, Sukhjeet felt petrified. As it happened, the vicious looking dog was highly trained and wouldn't maul its detainees unnecessarily but this was little consolation for Sukhjeet as he lay captive in the river, deemed impotent by its unnerving snarling and watchful, beady eyes. However, there was also a small but undeniable dose of relief. He had tried his best to enact the grand plan and now if he was deported back home what could he do about it? Perhaps it would be fine. Perhaps the paranoia about Inspector Baldev's Singh's devious intentions for a future re-arrest were overhyped. Maybe he could carry on his life and be with Anita after all? After a minute or two of this alternative future flashing before Sukhjeet's eyes, the dog inexplicably leapt off him, heading further into the river. There was a splash or two and then the next thing Sukhjeet heard was a loud thud, followed immediately by a high-pitched yelp. Fearing the worst but too fazed for his imagination to conjure up an image of what that might even be, Sukhjeet was finally free to drag himself into a sitting position. When he turned around, he was stunned by what he saw. There was Sajed, back into waist deep water, only a few metres away, smashing a sizeable rock repeatedly against the dog's head. He sat watching the surreal scene, not knowing whether to be terrified or grateful. In the moonlight, blood and bone fragments could be seen flying through the air, as Sajed manically finished the job that was already clearly finished, his beard waving around wildly as he did so. Though it was over in thirty seconds, it seemed to last forever, strike after strike after strike. However, when he did finally consider the job done, Sajed threw the rock into the river and extended his hand to Sukhjeet, helping him up to his feet. It was only now that Sukhjeet realised how badly his knee was injured. His leg buckled as soon as he put any weight on it and he shrieked in pain. Impulsively, Sajed put Sukhjeet's arm around his shoulders, supporting him so he could hop across the river on his one good leg.

As they approached the other side, Iqbal also ventured back into the river to prop up Sukhjeet's other side. Fortunately, tall reeds and thick vegetation provided them with excellent cover. They made their way about a hundred yards into the forest before Sukhjeet insisted they stop. The hopping itself was physically exhausting, plus his injured knee was jolting agonisingly every time he hopped. They crouched low to the ground and listened, as Sukhjeet caught his breath. Various male voices could be heard repeatedly shouting, 'Aleksei, Aleksei', presumably the dog's name. They wouldn't find him anytime soon though. Sajed had made sure of that by pushing its bloodied corpse into the fastest flowing part of the river. The fugitives, for that is what they certainly felt themselves to be now, waited silently, listening to the voices and praying that they wouldn't get any louder. Thankfully, they didn't. After about twenty minutes, the voices began to tail off and eventually the flashlights came back into view, this time ascending back up the valley.

'Thanks,' said Sukhjeet. *'I would have been arrested if*

it wasn't for you. It was very brave of you to come back to help me.'

'What would have happened, what could have happened or what did actually happen, these things are all in the hands of Allah. It is nothing to do with us.' He then put his hand on Sukhjeet's shoulder before continuing, 'And as for bravery, remember what I said to you. We Pashtuns are not scared of anything. Anyway, if your childhood is in Afghanistan, rabid dogs are the least of what you have to learn to deal with, eh, Iqbal?'

'One hundred percent, Sajed brother.' Iqbal nodded.

'Now, Mister Sukhjeet Singh, let's tie up that knee with something so we can get ourselves to the meeting point and make the phone-call. I am seriously cold.'

❖ ❖ ❖

11B. Wolverhampton, England: Feb 2017

Saturday was always peak business for the gargantuan Indian superstore on Dudley Road, just a stone's throw from the largest of the half-dozen gurdwaras in the city. 'Sohal Supermarket' had dominated the groceries market in this part of Wolverhampton for decades, successfully fighting off stiff competition from the mainstream supermarket chains that had all tried to open local branches but ultimately accepted defeat and moved on. The formula was unbeatable. Every staff member spoke at least one Indian language, predominantly Punjabi but Hindi, Urdu and Gujerati were also covered. Even the most obscure Indian cooking ingredient, fresh or preserved, was available in abundance. Once here to procure these otherwise scarce items, the convenience of then picking up slightly over-priced everyday supplies like milk and bread was then just too tempting. Furthermore, it was a social occasion. Religious ballads were played over loudspeakers in the mornings, morphing seamlessly into popular Punjabi bhangra music as the day progressed. Regular customers bumped into each other in the aisles and queues, exchanging greetings and catching up on events since their last meeting, which had probably also taken place in that same aisle, surrounded by mountains of tamarind tins and pickled ginger jars. The absolute clincher was the promise that an undisclosed proportion of the profits would be donated to the local gurdwara. Spending your money here was, in fact, charity!

As Sukhjeet walked into the store, shuffling past the crowd fighting over baskets from the rapidly depleting stack by the door, the first thing that hit him was the intensity of the aromas. Each step led him past a different dustbin sized container of freshly ground spice, stirring memories he didn't know he even had stored. Memories of tightly gripping his father's little finger as they navigated through the packed markets of Amritsar, stocking up on sacks of rice and spices for yet another upcoming special occasion. Fearful, as everyone seemed to tower over him but fascinated by the sights and sounds of this new, magical world.

Sukhjeet joined the queue for the till, which stretched down the brightly coloured toiletries, household goods and tupperware aisle, all the way to the butchery section at the back of the store. '100% JATKA MEAT,' proclaimed the large sign in capitalised English, Punjabi and Hindi, proudly boasting that the meat here was not prepared in the Islamic halal tradition, which is forbidden for Sikhs and also generally unpopular with other non-Muslim communities from India. He didn't mind the long wait, for the Punjabi radio was keeping him entertained. A chat-show was being broadcast, discussing the prevalence of fraudulent fortune-tellers from India, Pakistan and Bangladesh, operating across UK cities, duping vulnerable individuals into parting with significant sums of cash in exchange for ridding them of their woes. Anything was supposedly achievable, for a price: guaranteed reversal of bad-spells; solving of marital issues or a couple's inability to conceive; restraining troublesome in-laws; and, completely ridiculously, even cancer treatment. Listeners called in and regaled their distressing stories of exploitation and this was interspersed with somewhat poorly matched Punjabi dance numbers from the eighties. It surprised Sukhjeet to learn that this type of scam, common back in India, had even made its way across the Seven Seas. Even more astonishing was how lax the British authorities had evidently been with any sort of intervention to put a stop to it. Was it that they just weren't plugged into ethnic communities enough to even know it was going on, or was it a conscious policy? Perhaps an implicit insistence that these communities clean up their own dirt? He concluded it was probably a mixture of both, just as he reached the till, empty handed.

'*Yes brother, can I help you?*' asked the young attendant in Punjabi, the subtle mispronunciation of key consonants instantly giving him him away as a kid born and brought up in England.

'Do you have calling cards to India please? With a freephone number.' Sukhjeet responded in English, stressing the fact that the dial-up number must be free, exactly as explained by his flatmate, Raj.

'How much credit?

'Err...'

'Take this one. Five pounds, it's two and half pence per minute to India if you use the freephone number. And before you ask, yes, it works from a payphone bruv.'

'Thanks,' said Sukhjeet, handing over the exact change in a handful of coins, which the teenager accepted surprisingly happily, methodically separating out the denominations and diligently depositing them into their correct compartments within the cash register. Sukhjeet headed unhurriedly out of the store, head down, carefully removing the cellophane wrapper from the card, almost accidentally walking into an elderly lady hobbling into the store through the exit doors. It felt remarkable that this simple card was the key to hearing his parents' voices again. He did the sums. Two hundred minutes' worth of voice credit seemed like an infinite amount of time after two years without any communication with them whatsoever.

As he approached the payphone about a hundred yards away, the fluttering in his heart started to grow more intense. He was undoubtedly excited but also felt increasingly nervous, almost wishing the booth was occupied so it would buy him some time. His breathing was heavier now and he felt warm despite the crisp chill in the air. Unusually, the payphone was empty, so Sukhjeet stepped into it, simultaneously unzipping his jacket a little as he did so. He stood still, contemplating, leaning against the phone. It was dawning on him how significant these next few moments of his life could be and the more he thought about it the more he froze. Eventually, for lack of other options, he managed to motivate himself with positive thoughts about how everything would be fine, inhaled deeply and got ready to make the call. He had been in the booth for over ten minutes now and as he turned to face the phone, he noted how the condensation from his breath was starting to fog up the glass window panes.

When he did finally pick up the receiver, he almost immediately depressed the hook-switch with his other hand. He was still scared. In fact, he was petrified of bad news. Literally anything could have happened back home and this is the first he would hear about it. He leaned against the side of the booth and looked upwards. 'Sexual services' calling cards were stuffed into the creases where the booth's aluminium roof joined with the main structure. Sukhjeet stared, straight through the metal, into the sky, past the clouds and out into space, towards whomever was out there listening. And he prayed. It surprised him to know that he even believed in God anymore but he clearly did and right now he needed Him. He needed Him to tell Sukhjeet it was all OK back home and that his parents were absolutely fine. He wouldn't be able to cope with bad news, not when he was so powerless to help. It would break him.

As he looked back down, he saw an ant crawling up the side of the booth, slipping repeatedly when it encountered the fresh, wet condensation. Doggedly, it repeated its attempts, each time with more gusto, until eventually it made it past the wet patch back onto dry glass. Tiny little legs, surely exhausted from the obvious exertion, didn't even stop to take a momentary rest. No sooner was the ant on dry glass than it resumed its journey, now at breakneck speed, seemingly making up for the time lost overcoming the unexpected obstacle earlier.

Sukhjeet snapped himself out of his trance and took another consciously deep, nasal inhalation of breath. Exhaling with an exaggeratedly forceful puff out his mouth, he stood upright, released the hook switch and started resolutely punching in the long sequence of numbers. First the freephone access number, then the PIN from the card, which he had to scratch to reveal, followed finally by his home telephone number. Sukhjeet pressed the receiver tight against his ear, for he was struggling to hear clearly, the deep thumping of his heart deafening him. His mother answered, 'hello.' Sukhjeet tried to speak but nothing came out. *Sat Sri Akal ji, who is it?'* came her voice again, in Punjabi this time. Once again, he tried to speak, this time managing a choked splutter. And then there was complete silence, as time stood still for them both. For fear of unbearable disappointment, it took immense strength for his mother to dare hope it could be her son, alive and well. *'Sukhi, my son, is that you?*

Tears streamed down Sukhjeet's cheeks but somehow, he managed to restrain from turning into a sobbing wreck on the phone. *'Yes mom, it's me, Sukhi.'*

'Vaheguru, a million thanks to you, Vaheguru. Thank-you for keeping my son safe. Sukhi, you don't know how

happy I am to hear your voice.'

'*Mom, I missed you both so much.'* He paused and took a breath, wiping tears away with his sleeve. '*How is....'* he braced himself and continued....'*how is Daddy Ji?'* Silence ensued. Sukhjeet asked more insistently. '*Mom, how is Daddy Ji?'*

His knees nearly buckled with relief as he heard his father on the line. '*Son, it's Daddy here. Say something, let me hear your voice.'*

'*Daddy Ji?'*

'*Vaheguru, Vaheguru, Vaheguru. Thank you Vaheguru. Son, I told you Vaheguru would keep you safe.'* Sukhjeet had never heard such overt elation in his father's voice. He looked upwards towards the cosmos again, and under his breath said, '*Vaheguru – thank you.'*

In their excitement, his parents both started firing out questions at the same time, before realising that they were bombarding him and calming down to a more measured conversation, each quizzing him in turn, with the phone clearly on loudspeaker. He regaled a much-sanitised version of his epic journey. There was no benefit in upsetting them with the harrowing elements. So, he omitted the encounter with the border guards and dog at the Slovak border and the knee injury that still gave him difficulties. In the version he told his parents, the next part of the journey consisted of a comfortable train ride across Austria. Partly true but he had, in fact, travelled on the outside of the train, balanced precariously atop the carriage coupling on his one good leg, hanging on for dear life with fingers that had lost all sensation from the cold. Had it not been for Sajed and Iqbal physically holding him upright when his leg started cramping, he would certainly have fallen off. Another unidentified, dead migrant, to be stumbled across in some European field by a dog walker or rambler. Like the one Iqbal had discovered as they trudged across the snow-covered forest of the National Park, after their river crossing. With only moonlight as illumination, he had spotted what seemed like a pair of boots abandoned at the side of the path. As they looked far superior to the fraying trainers he was wearing, he had walking over to retrieve them, only to distressingly discover that they were still attached to their owner, who was otherwise buried in the frozen snow. The trio never discussed that incident, erasing it from their memories as best they could. The very real risk of their also soon ending up as abandoned, frozen nobodies somewhere, was too demoralising to dwell on.

He didn't tell his parents about the nightmares he still suffered from. How he had now learned to wake himself up at will, as the only way to escape the terrifying memories tormenting him in his sleep. His mind played cruel tricks on him by blending his traumatic life experiences with even darker possibilities. He dreamed of being incarcerated in Russia, stripped naked in a frozen cell, beaten by Inspector Baldev Singh. He dreamed of Sajed being caught and deported back to Afghanistan, where he is then arrested and punished by the very Taliban he had been trying to escape. Sajed's father, whom Sukhjeet imagined to be an aging man, with a henna dyed beard, wearing an Afghan pakol hat, begging the cruel executioners to kill him instead. Explaining to them that he was the one who had worked with the Americans as an interpreter, that he was the one who had insisted on Sajed escaping the country and that hence his son shouldn't pay the price. Sukhjeet always woke up before the beheading, stark upright in bed, relieved that he didn't have to witness such a brutal atrocity, even in his sleep.

No, there was nothing to be gained by exposing his parents to the griefs he had endured. Much like they didn't expose him to their own woeful experiences. They omitted tales of the police harassment for many months after his 'disappearance'. They missed out stories of the agent demanding more money to guarantee safe passage for their son. They downplayed the loneliness they felt every single day of their lives and how his mother still set his place at their dinner table every night. No, this was an occasion to be joyful. They had all come through the darkness and there would be better days ahead. Sukhjeet talked of his work, how his engineering had come in useful after all and how he was now making reasonable money. He described how he lived with fellow Punjabis and boasted about the influence of that community in the local area, describing the glamour of the golden domed and marble clad local gurdwaras in detail.

However, the irony was that though he was happy to bury his darkest moments to protect his parent's feelings, he felt genuinely saddened by the compulsion he felt to hide his happiest too. Zainab was not mentioned.

SECTION 12:
SECOND CHANCE

'Life can only be understood backwards, but it must be lived forwards.' Soren Kierkegaard.

12A. Sangatte Calais,
France: May 2015

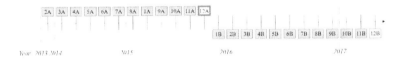

'**S**omeone really is in a celebration mood today,' said Sajed jovially, as he watched Iqbal neatly arranging the multitude of foil containers on the concrete and carefully removing the lids. Appetising fragrances started to flood out and Sukhjeet felt his hungry stomach gurgle impulsively in response. In a surprising act of generosity, Iqbal had volunteered to purchase a selection of nibbles from the short, plump, bespectacled

Pakistani man who, judging from the length of the leading up to his estate car, was clearly doing very well sell-
ing his wife's home cooked selection of hot and cold food
items out the boot. From snacks to full meals, including
curries, rice, naans, desserts and even authentic masala
chai, he had it all. They had spotted him parked on a grass
verge, just outside Sangatte refugee camp. This happened
to be precisely opposite the disused factory car-park
where Sukhjeet had been instructed to wait this particular afternoon, in order to be picked-up for the final leg of
his journey. The dreaded, high-security Channel Tunnel
transit was now the only remaining obstacle separating
him from his final destination. The Afghans, on the other
hand, had no real reason to be in that spot today. But
whilst they waited for local traffickers to generate English Channel crossing options and gather pricing quotes
for them, they had little else to do. So, seemingly by way
of sheer boredom, combined with an understandable
curiosity as to how Sukhjeet's 'deluxe package' transportation would pan out, here they were too. Sukhjeet
was certainly grateful for the company and indeed the
security in numbers. Even for someone like him, fully
capable of handling himself in a hot corner, Sangatte was
an intimidating place. The camp was segregated into
areas of nationality-based domination and gangs of often
drug crazed enforcers armed with machetes and crow-
bars roamed the streets looking for anyone that didn't
belong in their sector. The primary risk, stemming from
accidentally venturing into a 'foreign zone', where you
wouldn't have paid your protection racket fees, was rob-
bery. However, most of the refugees in the camp were
forced to keep their valuables on their person, for lack of
anywhere secure to store them and not being around

anyone they could trust to guard them at their tent or shack. So, the impact of being robbed could be catastrophic, potentially involving the loss of all your cash as well as every other valuable you owned. Valuables which could otherwise be very usefully pawned at a later stage if the need to generate further cash arose, which it often did. Understandably then, though very unwisely as it transpired, victims would resist and these robberies often turned out to be incredibly violent episodes. Though subsequently gossiped about incessantly around the camp, these frequent, highly unpleasant incidents would hardly ever be investigated by the police or reported in the local media, Little surprise then, that they continued unabated, the 'residents' of the camp resigning themselves to the fact this was simply part and parcel of life at the infamous Sangatte camp.

With the sun shining brightly and trees starting to blossom, those freezing nights in Eastern Europe really did seem like a lifetime away. *'Sukhjeet brother is leaving us today. I thought we should have something special for our final meal together,'* said Iqbal, explaining his rationale for the purchase.

Sukhjeet was touched. *'It's not our final meal. We will meet again on the other side and that's when I will repay the favour.'*

'Insha'Allah. OK, so, we have some tandoori chicken, but it was halal so I bought veg samosas and also pakoras for Sukhjeet brother.'

Sukhjeet smiled. He was touched by the consideration and also pleased he had managed to impart something about his own culture to the Afghan duo. *'Brothers, we have been through so much together. I wouldn't even be here today if you hadn't helped me. Truth be told, I really am beyond caring about cultural differences and religious requirements. The only thing that matters is the loved ones around you and reciprocating the respect they give you. So, if it's good enough for you, it's good enough for me.'* He picked up a lukewarm, bright red chicken drumstick and bit into it, savouring the explosion of familiar flavours in his mouth. But the aroma and longed-for taste of home brought with it all the memories of his family that he had pushed to the back of his mind. He wondered how his parents would be coping with absolutely no idea about his progress, for he had zero confidence in the agent keeping them abreast of developments. Nevertheless, he remained committed to honouring his promise not to call until the full two years since his departure were up: February 2017. And what about Anita? God, he missed her. His eyes started to well up and Iqbal noticed him wiping tiny tears away with his sleeve.

'Too spicy for your weak Indian taste buds, Sukhjeet?' If Iqbal's intention was to distract him and lighten the mood, it worked. Sukhjeet couldn't help but swallow his grief and start chuckling. The others laughed with him, as they continued to tuck into the remaining, indulgent platter.

With the foil trays completely emptied out, Sukhjeet grabbed a piece of kitchen towel and wiped the corner of his mouth. As he did so, his fingers stumbled across the thin but pronounced swelling along the scar that had now formed on his face. He lingered on it, stroking it repeatedly along its entire length. Part of him was in pure awe at the incredible ability of the human body to recover from trauma. But a lot of him was still just bitter about the needless nature of all this suffering. What if he hadn't called that particular gathering at the university that fateful day? What if he had toned down his rhetoric at previous meetings and not attacked the role of the police quite so directly? Could he have gone for an online campaign instead and possibly achieved just as much reach and impact, if not more, without being so visible as the unequivocal leader of the crusade? Hell, what if he hadn't even bothered with all this human rights awareness malarkey at all?

Again, it fell to Iqbal to break the ensuing silence. *'It looks a lot better now Sukhjeet. When you first took the bandage off back in Ukraine, there was a lot of yellow puss coming out. But it's just a scar now. Can't even see it with a little beard growth. I know why you are sad but there is no need to worry.'* He smirked before continuing. *'A handsome man like you will still definitely have all the sexy white girls chasing after you in England.'*

It starkly dawned on Sukhjeet how much he would miss Iqbal's cheeky smile and ability to introduce much needed humour to even the darkest moments. As for Sajed, the man had risked everything to save Sukhjeet, despite the fact that he had been pretty much a stranger. How would he ever be able to repay the debt he felt he owed him? Putting one each of his hands on the shoulders of the two men, Sukhjeet replied, just about managing to stay composed. *'I am really going to miss you both.'* No further words were exchanged on the subject and none were needed. The Afghans both simply reached over and each squeezed his hands in response.

About an hour after they had finished eating, they saw the much awaited 'EMRT – East Midlands Refrigerated Transport' lorry turn into the car-park. The driver took a while to park, meticulously backing into the far corner from where they could load the rear without being seen from the road. Once he turned the engine off, the driver proceeded to speak on a mobile phone for a few minutes before popping open the cab door and jumping down. He was a gaunt, exceedingly pale man in his fifties, with a heavily wrinkled face and completely bald head. Without getting too close to the three men, he shouted out in a thick eastern European accent, 'one of you is Sukhjeet Singh?'

'Yes, sir,' replied Sukhjeet, unnecessarily raising his hand at the same time.

Sukhjeet began walking towards the driver. He was still limping noticeably, but the sharp stabbing pain each time he took a step had now subsided to a large degree. Surprising, given the only medical care he had received in the intervening time was from a fellow migrant – another 'donkey' - whom he had met in one of the numerous, squalid transit houses he had stayed at within Germany. The man, professing to be a Sri Lankan doctor, had been very pleasant but was entirely unwilling to share any details about his motivations for undertaking this onerous migration journey. Doubtful as to whether he really was a qualified medical practitioner at first, Sukhjeet had quickly realised his options were to let him attend to the injury or continue to put up with the excruciating pain. So, upon the doctor's own recommendation, Sukhjeet had anaesthetised himself with a half-bottle of whiskey prior to the examination. Given he was previously a teetotaller, this worked effectively in not only alleviating much of the piercing pain during the examination but also relieving him of most of his other senses. However, even numbed in this manner, he could still feel a deep, grating vibration all the way up his leg and into his hips whenever the doctor bent his knee back and forth. It was diagnosed as a partial tear of the patellar tendon, the optimal next steps for which were an MRI scan and then quite possibly minor surgery. Clearly, none of this fancy healthcare was an option, so they improvised a knee support and Sukhjeet was given some stretches and self-physio to perform daily instead.

'OK. Who are others? I take only you.' Sukhjeet was snapped back from his recollections by the driver.

'Yes. Only I am going. These are my friends; they came to say goodbye.'

The driver looked understandably unconvinced and highly apprehensive at the sight of this heavily bearded farewell party. However, they quickly got down to business. The driver, Jan, who turned out to be Polish, opened up the rollup door at the rear of the trailer. Immediately, the men were hit with a blast of chilled air. This giant fridge seemed initially to be completely full to the brim with boxes of refrigerated meat, until Jan shuffled a few of the central boxes out the way to reveal a small vacant space, sufficient for one adult human's standing room only. He handed Sukhjeet a thick woollen blanket and gestured for him to take up his position and then wrap the blanket around himself, before explaining that Jan would then be stacking up the meat boxes again, literally burying Sukhjeet alive.

'No problem. Only about four hours. And you can breathe no problem. Fresh air coming in.'

The Afghans looked absolutely petrified on Sukhjeet's behalf. Sajed stood staring blankly into the truck, without moving a muscle.

'*Brothers, look at these boxes. This truck is full of pork.*

It is haram for you. Perhaps that's why Allah arranged for you to travel a different way, eh? For a "kafir" like me though, it's fine.' He winked at the Afghans and tried to conjure up a smile. Putting on a brave face in this way was intended primarily to distract him from his own anxiety. *'Anyway, this driver is saying it will only be a four-hour journey and there is fresh air coming in to breathe.'* The Afghans barely spoke English and hence Sukhjeet figured it was highly unlikely they could understand Jan with his strong accent. So, he opted to translate for their benefit, hoping to put their minds at rest but also so that he might receive some reciprocal reassurance back from them. None was forthcoming.

'I don't think this is safe, Sukhjeet. What will happen if there is a delay, accident or you get stuck in here?'

'What could happen and what does actually happen, these things are all in the hands of Allah – it is nothing to do with us.' Sukhjeet's quote was a play on what Sajed had said to him after the incident with the dog at the Slovak border and Sajed recognised it immediately.

He mulled over it for a moment, before concluding there was no credible counter-argument. *'You are right. Allah Hafiz brother – may Allah protect you.'*

The three men hugged each other briefly and the Afghans then gave Sukhjeet a helpful lift up into the trailer. As he was being buried behind the boxes of meat, that last image of the Afghans was something he would never forget. Iqbal, grinning at him mischievously, his teeth stained red by the excessive food colouring on the chicken, and Sajed, unable to hide his tears but, nevertheless, enthusiastically waving goodbye. Within minutes, the job was done. The door rolled closed and Sukhjeet was plunged into total darkness which instantly made it feel far colder. He adjusted the blanket as best he could, pulling it up to cover his head, leaving only a small gap through which he would breathe. Seconds later, he heard the growl of the engine starting up and felt the truck start to move off towards the port. He was stressed. He knew that from the fact that he couldn't stop twitching. Purposefully trying to distract himself, he resurrected vague memories from a university lecture on refrigeration. Reminding himself of the science behind his current incarceration successfully occupied twenty minutes or so but the more he thought about it, the more adamantly he recalled that one of the core principles of fridges is that they are sealed. Why on earth would there be this supposed fresh air coming in?

Sukhjeet's recollections of the next few hours were a little hazy, consisting primarily of intense cold and almost continual, violent shivering. However, at a certain moment, very abruptly, he knew unequivocally that he was in the tunnel and moving aboard a train. The cooling unit was too noisy and his ears too numbed to actually hear anything but he could feel the rapid but smooth accelerations and decelerations without any road bumps. His present confinement didn't permit it but this was surely worthy of celebration. Despite all the odds and by successfully overcoming all the challenges that had been thrown his way, he had actually, really done it. Getting from Indian to Calais was a mind-blowing achievement in itself. But this? Wow! He had made it through the most sophisticated border security in the world without detection, first time. As if physically injected into him, relief gushed through his veins. He felt it make its way down his legs, calming the twitching; through his heart, slowing his heartbeat; and into his head, inducing him into a heady sleep.

Sukhjeet definitely felt the first slap and recognised it as such but it wasn't enough to fully wake him. The second, however, felt much harder. Or perhaps he was just primed by the first? Jan dragged him upright, helped him down, out of the truck, from his slumped position amongst the boxes, and handed him a bottle of water. Feeling instantly unsteady on his feet, he sat down on the grass, before starting to take in his surroundings, squinting, as his eyes got accustomed to broad daylight again. So, this must be it; England. The sun was starting to set. The same sun that shone in France, back in Punjab and all those countries he had traversed. The sky was still blue, peppered with fluffy white clouds. Green fields spread out as far as he could see, just like home. He heard the same familiar birdsong in the air, as he remained sat, motionless, next to the truck. He took in big gasps of air, only now beginning to realise how breathless he was, having been partially starved of oxygen for the past few hours. As he slowly recovered, coming around fully to his senses, piercingly painful pins and needles started to replace the numbness of his feet.

Seeing Sukhjeet looking the right colour again, the blue tinges having vanished from his lips, Jan threw down his cigarette, crushed it under his foot and walked over to his human cargo, extending his arm to help him to stand up. He took a few photos on his phone of Sukhjeet standing in front of a road sign pointing to some village, supposedly one and a quarter mile away. The name of the village, which Sukhjeet couldn't later recall, seemed too bizarre to be real, like it had been plucked out of some fantasy novel set in the middle ages. Finished with his evidence gathering, Jan extended his arm once again, this time to shake Sukhjeet's hand. 'Welcome to England Mister Sukhjeet Singh. My job is done. You are on your own now.' He handed Sukhjeet an envelope but before Sukhjeet could even respond or open it, the driver was walking back towards the driver cab. 'Good luck!' he shouted, as he looked around at Sukhjeet one last time whilst ascending the ladder steps, before climbing in and slamming the heavy cab door behind him with a clunk. Sukhjeet was smothered with thick diesel fumes as the engine revved, the indicator started flashing and eventually the truck crawled away down the country lane. He opened the envelope to confirm but already knew what would be inside. He unravelled a few blank pieces of A4 paper and out dropped a fake British passport and UK driving licence. There were also the agreed details of a local, Punjabi contact that he would need to call in order to transport him to some small town a few hours' drive away, called Wolverhampton. Here, for a not inconsiderable fee, he would apparently be introduced to a few gang masters that could get him ongoing, paid work.

In the end, the agent had ultimately delivered on most of what he had promised. Sure, there had undeniably been considerable embellishment regarding the ease and comfort with which Sukhjeet would be transported but he was here now and everything that had gone before seemed like water under the bridge. But really, this was all small consolation. It struck Sukhjeet that the real graft would start now. He still needed to build an entire life here, whilst being handicapped by his alien status in this foreign country. So, justifiably nervous and feeling lonelier than he had ever felt since first arriving in Russia months ago, he took his first steps into this new life. However, though he was certainly lonely, he was not despondent. After all, despite everything seemingly being stacked against him, he had made it this far and was absolutely determined to let nothing stop him now.

12B. Wolverhampton, England: Apr 2017

Sukhjeet knew only an hour or so of pleasant, morning rays remained for him to bask in, before the sun would disappear behind the adjoining terrace house, plunging their little garden into shade for the remainder of the day. It didn't bother him though. It might be north facing, it might be tiny, but it was a garden and it was all theirs. No longer than eight foot each side, an aging, wood panel fence encased this little outdoor alcove, its multitude of loosened edging strips drooping like the branches of a weeping willow. Weathered paving stones, originally grey but now stained to a murky brown, covered the first two thirds of the garden. Grass peered out from all the joins with an uncanny uniformity, forming an unkempt, natural, outdoor chessboard, albeit with only twelve squares. At the end was some shrubbery, completely neglected by the previous tenants. Aggressive weeds ominously wrapped their thorny stems around the otherwise impressively tall rose bush and sunflower plants, in what seemed like a coordinated effort to suffocate them from all sides. 'Are you sure you are from a farming family, Sukhi? You have been staring at that tiny patch of vegetation for a month now, putting off sorting it out.' Zainab was looking down as she spoke, gingerly descending down the slightly loose concrete steps leading from the kitchen into the garden, her facial expression clearly displaying the deep concentration required for her to manoeuvre whilst balancing the large stainless-steel tray holding two cups of tea and a plate of biscuits.

Zainab delicately placed the tray down on the small wrought iron table, relieved she had managed to navigate the various obstacles without any spillages. They had found that table abandoned in the garden. It had been in a sorry state but after an entire day of their both industriously sanding, painting and polishing, it had come up an absolute treat. Sukhjeet pulled back the spare dining chair he had already carried outside just for her and she sat down next to him.

Acknowledging Zainab's arrival yet further, he also turned off the small portable radio he had been listening to. Sport Midlands FM had been playing, the commentator discussing Wolverhampton Wanderers' upcoming matches and reviewing their devastating season so far. Languishing near the bottom of the Championship, their 2-0 defeat a few days prior at the hands of albeit divisional leaders Brighton-and-Hove had also been the talk of the building site. For a team that seemed to be perpetually losing, at least for the six months or so Sukhjeet had followed them, 'Wolves' somehow managed to inspire incredibly loyal support from its fanbase. The town would be alive on match-days, a sea of orange scarves, with old and young, of all colours and creeds, converging from far afield in cars and buses, then excitedly marching the final pedestrianised stretch down to the impressive Molineux stadium and even filling the town's pubs and bars with joviality after matches, regardless of the result. Back in Punjab, Sukhjeet had been an avid fan of Real Madrid, idolising Cristiano Ronaldo. But there was something about the proximity of this local team, the intimacy of its failures and emotional highs of the fans when they enjoyed their rare successes, that he desperately wanted to be part of. He was beginning to take a keen interest in their progress and was now hardly even following the bigger European level teams.

The slight chill in the spring air, despite the sunshine, caught Zainab off guard and she adjusted her dressing gown a little, wrapping it tighter across her neck and chest. Her long hair wafted in the breeze, still damp from her shower. 'So, what now?' she quizzed, abruptly ending his daydream about attending a future Wolves match.

'What? In life?' replied Sukhjeet, in a genuine attempt to obtain some more clarity on the somewhat vague question. He liked it when her hair was wet. The bright shine and slightly unkempt fall of her curls gave her an air of youthfulness that Sukhjeet always felt was well suited to her fantastically sprightly personality.

'No, silly. What are the plans for our day off today? Looks like emir sahib wants to put off the gardening again.'

'No point starting that today.' Sukhjeet looked up at the sky, raising his hand against his forehead to block out the glare of the sun from his eyes. It's going to rain, look at the clouds moving in.'

'Wow. Engineer, farmer and weather-man. Emir sahib really is multi-talented!' As always, despite her attempt to maintain an expressionless face, Zainab's sarcastic intent was exposed by the deep dimples that formed in her cheeks whenever she was trying to withhold laughter. Sukhjeet's slight annoyance at the suggestion that he wasn't pulling his weight with household chores quickly waned and he couldn't resist a smile, prompting Zainab to chuckle out loud. 'Don't worry. You had a tough week. Why don't you have this Sunday to completely relax? But if no work comes in next week for Saturday, then will you promise to sort the garden? Please. Summer is coming and I really want a nice place to sit and enjoy the three days of summer you get in this country every year.

'OK, fine.'

'Promise?'

'Yes sweetheart, I promise,' said Sukhjeet, leaning forward to give her right cheek a squeeze. Just at that moment, the peaceful suburban Sunday morning silence was abruptly interrupted by a short-lived but absolutely unmistakable beating of a drum.

'Did you hear that?' Zainab asked.

The drumbeat, though it had only lasted a few seconds, reverberated deep within Sukhjeet's chest. Not by virtue of its loudness or proximity, but because of its familiarity. His mind raced, desperately trying to match those unmistakable pulsations with some distant memory.

'You heard it right?' Zainab repeated. But before Sukhjeet could answer, the drums started again. This time, longer and louder. Now there was no mistaking as to what this was.

Sukhjeet adjusted himself on his seat, impulsively swivelling his whole body towards the direction of the noise. 'It's a ranjit nagara.'

'A what? The drum we can hear?'

'It's a big, special drum, called a ranjit nagara. Sikhs used to play it as they marched into battle.'

'Really? Cool. How come it is being played today?'

Sukhjeet looked pointlessly down at his watch. It told him the time - quarter to eleven, but he was actually trying to work out the date and his watch was no use for that. However, he quickly recalled that his payday envelope this Friday gone had '14th April' scrawled on the front. 'It is Vaisakhi this weekend, a big celebration for Sikhs.'

'Hold on, hold on. Don't tell me.' Zainab hesitated a moment before recalling the story that Sukhjeet had regaled to her a few times before. 'This is where the, I think, the...tenth Guru...' Her voice tailed off, looking for confirmation from Sukhjeet that she was on the correct track.

'Yes...exactly.'

'So, yes, the tenth guru, Guru Gobind Singh, gathered all his followers and created this new "Order" I think you called it; the Khalsa - the pure.'

'Wow. Impressive memory Zainab!'

She was smiling innocently, like a studious child who had just been praised by her teacher in class. 'I always remember that particular story. I told you right, "khalis" means pure in Arabic so the word sticks in my mind.' The beating of the drum was definitely getting louder now but was having to compete with the discordant noise from multiple, indecipherable loudspeakers bellowing. 'What's actually going on though?'

'It's a nagar kirtan. So, the all the local Sikhs will march through the neighbourhood in a long procession. The holy book – Guru Granth Sahib – will be transported along the whole route, probably inside a vehicle. Normally, the march is led by the panj pyare. These are five local Sikhs, on whom this special honour is bestowed. They will dress pretty much exactly how the Guru asked the first five initiated Khalsa Sikhs to dress all those years ago, when the Order was created, on the original Vaisakhi celebration in 1699.'

'Wow. That's so cool. I think they might come down our road, right? It's the only road wide enough to take a procession. Do people come out of their houses to watch?'

'Of course. In Punjab, all the householders line the streets with stalls to hand out drinks and snacks to the procession.'

Sukhjeet noticed Zainab disappearing into her own little world, looking blankly out past Sukhjeet towards the source of the noise, little movements of her eyes revealing that she was deep in thought about something. 'What you thinking Zainab?'

'I have an idea.' With that, she put her teacup on the tray and ran into the house, accidentally snagging one of her flip-flops on a step and almost tripping in the process.

'Careful! Where you going?' shouted Sukhjeet.

'Gimme two minutes.'

Clearly, whatever Zainab was thinking, it would entail

going outside to watch the nagar kirtan procession. Given the genuine threat of rain whilst they would be distracted out the front of the house, Sukhjeet opted to bring the tray in and move the chairs back to their home at the small two-man dining table in the kitchen. He slammed the rear door shut, kicking the lower part where the wood, swollen from all the recent downpours, was starting to catch the frame. It then took him a little while fiddling with the key before eventually managing to lock it. As he turned to hang the key on its dedicated little hook, his attention was caught by the tap handle. It must have come loose yet again and had been placed at on the sink drainer by Zainab, for Sukhjeet to reattach. Frustrated, he sighed and took a moment to look around the rest of the room. The loose sink splashboard tiles, the patches of blackened grout, the kitchen unit doors that didn't close properly, the chipped worktop surface, the cracked flooring. It was by far the worst room in the apartment. The singular bedroom with its en-suite bathroom and the small but cosy living room, were both actually fine, probably renovated within the last five years. But the kitchen was where Zainab spent so much of her time, the passionate cook that she was. It bothered Sukhjeet that this is all he could provide for her. Though, in his defence, it had been complicated. Despite his protestations, Zainab was not prepared to let Sukhjeet use his fake passport as his 'UK right-to-rent' documentation. That meant that they could secure a property based purely on Zainab's nursing salary, even though Sukhjeet was bringing in decent cash-in-hand wages. So, they were restricted to this; a single floor apartment in a converted terrace house. A young Chinese family lived upstairs, where the landlord had somehow managed to cram in another small apartment. That couple had their own private staircase access so rarely crossed paths with Sukhjeet or Zainab. In fact, most of the time, the only reason their presence was even known was the baby's crying or the parents' regular, screaming arguments. It had been the private outdoor space that had swung it for Zainab. Hailing from a desert, she loved the idea of sitting outside amongst greenery, sipping tea, like an English 'madam'. She would take any opportunity to sit there, even when the temperature really didn't warrant it. He suddenly felt a pang of guilt and promised himself that he would devote the following weekend to tidying up the garden, even doing the unthinkable and turning down work on Saturday if he had to.

He ventured further into the apartment when he almost bumped into Zainab rushing out the bedroom. 'Oh, you scared me,' she said, holding up her hand to her chest as she inhaled a deep breath to calm her nerves. 'I thought you were still in the garden. Anyway, what do you think?' she asked, performing a full twirl for him. Sukhjeet was completely lost for words. She was wearing a deep green coloured Punjabi style salwar kameez. It hugged her figure perfectly, following all the alluring curves of her body. Intricate gold embroidery adorned the hem and neckline. The matching glittery chunni, which Sikh women tend to wear more loosely over their heads, was pulled lower over her forehead and then tucked behind her ears, in the style that many Muslim women in Punjab would authentically tend to wear it. Even the colour of her heels matched the outfit, as did the bangles she had also donned. She looked simply stunning and caught Sukhjeet totally off guard.

Still gobsmacked, but keen to say something, Sukhjeet clutched at the first words that came to him. 'Errr...wow, what the hell?'

'That's not the response I was hoping for!' replied Zainab, her previous excitement visibly draining from her face.

Sukhjeet stepped forward, relying on impulse where trying to articulate his emotions into words was clearly failing him, again. He cupped Zainab's head with both his hands and kissed her on the forehead, dropping his arms to then embrace her tightly. Zainab reciprocated and they stood in silence, locked in a firm embrace. Having savouring the moment, it was Zainab who spoke. 'That's more like the reaction I expected, silly!'

Sukhjeet relaxed his grip and they pulled apart slightly. 'But why do you have this outfit?'

'Does it matter?'

'No, but...'

'I told you I had a Sikh doctor friend when I worked in Birmingham. We became really close in a short space of time and she invited me to her wedding. She took me shopping in Handsworth for an outfit to wear on the big day, helped me choose it, taught me about all the accessories and showed me how to wear everything properly.' As she spoke, she jangled her bangles and touched her earrings, further emphasising how much thought had gone into the various adornments.

'You look stunning, Zainab.'

'Aww, thanks.' She smiled and lowered her gaze, cheeks visibly blushing at the sheer rawness and intensity of the compliments. She tried to shuffle past him towards the kitchen but he blocked her way, gently pushing her up against the wall. She immediately sensed where this was headed. Surprised at the degree of impact

her dressing up had on Sukhjeet and managing to overcome her own desire to leverage it further, she wriggled
free from his grip. 'No, no, no. We need to go outside and
watch. Come on, honey.'

'But...'

'Later Sukhi. Come on!'

'OK, OK.' Regaining his composure, Sukhjeet went
into the bedroom to find a head covering, a necessity if
they were to join the procession. He walked back into
the kitchen, tying his bandana as he went, to find Zainab
frantically filling plastic cups from a jug of orange squash
and lining them up on the tray. She had also pulled out
a few bags of mini chocolates, left over from the very
small house-warming gathering they had held with some
of Zainab's friends when they first moved in. He stood at
the doorway, silently reflecting how well Zainab would
probably get on with his mother. As she rushed frantically about the kitchen in her Punjabi attire, rustling
up something from seemingly nothing, the ends of her
chunni floating behind her at each abrupt change of direction, he saw similarities between them he had never
noted before.

Outside, the noise of the loudspeakers was now
very close. The drums could be felt through the floor-
boards as well as heard. Zainab threw him the bags of
chocolates. 'Here, hold these. And grab my phone off the
counter, I want to take some photos.'

If it was loud inside, it was substantially louder
once they opened the front door and squeezed past the
wheelie bins and onto the pavement. Sukhjeet glanced
upwards to spot two Chinese faces at the window, one
atop the other, holding their net curtains aside, ner-

vously investigating the commotion on the street.

The procession could be seen approaching and was now only a few hundred yards away. Overwhelming sounds emanated in all directions. A loud drum beat, an uncoordinated array of religious ballads being blasted over different loudspeakers attached to vehicles, the congregation singing, occasional horning of vehicles, stewards shouting instructions over handheld loudspeakers, all merging to create a truly tremendous cacophony. Zainab was excited beyond words. 'Wow!' was the only thing she could muster up, which she shouted loudly into Sukhjeet's ear. Swapping the tray of drinks for the phone in his hands, she started preparing the device to record the proceedings.

At the helm was a black, pick-up style Humvee vehicle, evidently cleaned and polished especially for the occasion, chrome fixtures glistening whenever they caught the sun reappearing from behind a cloud. Orange stickers and sashes adorned the entire vehicle but the most striking feature was two crossed flagpoles, each about 2 metres long, tied neatly to the front bumper and radiator. On the end of each one was a Nishan Sahib – the triangular, orange Sikh flag, with the poles themselves also entirely covered with orange draping. On its rear, the vehicle held the drum – the ranjit nagara. It was way larger than Zainab had expected, for Sukhjeet had not explained that it was historically carried into battle on elephant-back! Over a metre in diameter, the drum was being played enthusiastically by a young, heavily built Sikh man, dressed in Western clothes, with a large, dome shaped, black turban and wearing a luminous orange 'STAFF' vest.

Next came half a dozen men and women, in a mix of western and Punjabi clothing, diligently sweeping the road with brooms. Slightly perplexed at first, it only took a glance from Zainab over and above her phone's screen before she realised that they were clearing debris just ahead of the main procession, led by the five Khalsa Sikhs that Sukhjeet had talked of earlier. All five were impressively bearded Sikh men, dressed identically: bare footed, thereby explaining the sweeping; with orange robes and turbans; blue sashes around their waist; white cotton scarves loosely around their necks and each holding a full-length curved edge sword proudly ahead of them. They were flanked by one further man on either side who walked a few steps ahead, identically dressed but each holding an identical flag to the ones on the Humvee. Following this came the centrepiece, a large purpose-built float, enclosed on all sides with floor to ceiling glass, partially open on the sides, swathed in fresh flower arrangements. Large banners across the top were emblazoned in Punjabi but with helpful English translations. 'Recognise the human race as one' on the front side and 'He alone is a true warrior who fights against evil' down the nearside edge. Inquisitive about these seemingly universally applicable messages, Zainab was a little disappointed she couldn't see what was on the opposite side. Inside the float, at the front but facing rearwards, was a group of seated men, dressed in plain white kurta pyjamas, with black waistcoats and orange turbans, playing harmoniums and tablas. During the few minutes whilst the float passed by and their music and voices could actually be heard, they offered a soothing interlude to the otherwise uncoordinated noise of jubilation and celebration that filled the air. At the rear of the float but facing forward was clearly the centrepiece, marked by an ornate golden dome on the roof of the float itself, directly above its position. It was a raised platform, decked in multiple layers of colourful and fabulously embroidered cloths. An older man, who was similarly dressed to the musicians, was sat at the head of this platform, energetically waving over it a large fan made seemingly of strands of animal hair. Zainab was intrigued as to what was happening here but didn't want to disturb her video recording whilst turning to quiz Sukhjeet. So, she made a mental note to query it later. There was one last showpiece element remaining, ahead of the thousands of local Sikhs who were marching behind in the procession, kept hemmed into an orderly advance by dozens more luminous vested 'staff' holding up ropes to corral everyone into the road and stop them wandering onto the pavements. The moving martial arts display was captivating to watch. Sikhs, aged anywhere from ten to possibly as high as sixty, boys, girls, men and women, dressed in long blue robes, some with matching blue turbans whilst others wearing blue bandanas, displayed their skills with swords, daggers, maces, shields and wooden staffs as they pounced energetically around an area which the crowd wisely dared not encroach upon.

Zainab, satisfied she had filmed suitably comprehensively, turned to face Sukhjeet, who was stood lost in his own world. 'Hey. That was amazing!' she said, excitedly. 'I think I got some good footage.' But before he had a chance to respond, she remembered the tray of drinks and chocolates he was still holding. 'Oh, let me hand these out.' With that, she grabbed Sukhjeet's arm and pulled him closer to the crowd, before starting to hand out the squash. The supplies didn't last long. The tray was soon clear apart from the empties, most people having drunk the contents in one gulp and handed back the plastic cup. Zainab grabbed the bags of chocolates and tore them open, before taking them to the crowds, kneeling a little in a clear indication that these were intended for the children. A little girl, no more than 5 years old, sheepishly took two chocolates, ready to return the extra one if she was scolded. Soon realising that no reprimand was forthcoming, a huge smile erupted across her cheeks. 'Thanks aunty' she said to Zainab. Her chubby cheeks, rosy red from the slight chill in the air, were too cute for Zainab to resist squeezing.

Her mother, a tall woman with sharp facial features and exuding a very natural beauty, dressed in a colourful Punjabi suit but covered with a black, heavy winter jacket, also started to smile. The resemblance between mother and child became starker as she did so. 'Thanks. She is such a greedy pig, aren't you Gagan?' she mused, looking down at her daughter.

Zainab heard a feint 'no I'm not,' as the pair were shunted along by the crowd. Then, just within earshot, she saw the girl tug her mother's hand and say, 'mummy, aunty was wearing same colour as me.'

Zainab turned to face Sukhjeet, cocked her head to the side and fluttered her eyelashes whilst pouting her lips to silently say, 'soooooooo cute'.

Though he read her lips perfectly, Sukhjeet drew his own conclusion of the underlying meaning. 'I want one' is what he took it to mean, and more importantly, 'I want one with you.' He smiled back enthusiastically.

As the procession dwindled, now consisting only of the elderly who were trailing behind and yet more vested 'staff' busily engaged with litter collection duties, Zainab grabbed the tray from Sukhjeet and walked back into the house. Sukhjeet stood still on the pavement, grappling with a torrent of conflicting emotions. Undoubtedly still embittered by how life had treated him, his resentment clashed with a dose of gratefulness. Memories of that day standing nervously in the phone booth flashed in front of him. But, the overriding recollection from that day was of relief and sheer joy at hearing his parent's voices. Meeting Zainab; he couldn't even describe how content that made him. Every day he woke up appreciative for whatever circumstance and fate had brought them together. Indeed, as the Guru Granth Sahib had driven past moments earlier, in its regally decorated golden-domed float, he had impulsively bowed his head, closed his eyes and whispered, *'Vaheguru, thank you,'* under his breath. In the intensity of that moment, he had even momentarily considered breaking his self-imposed ban on ever entering a gurdwara and actually joining the procession to its conclusion at the largest gurdwara in Wolverhampton. But, with the procession and the devotees disappearing into the distance, he felt his desire to join them also start to ebb.

After a few more moments staring blankly ahead and trying but failing to makes sense of his feelings, Sukhjeet turned to go back inside. But, after only a few steps, he was confronted by Zainab coming back out of the house, wearing a coat over her own outfit and holding his jacket in her hand. She held it out for him. 'You should go' she said.

'But…'

'Come on, I will go with you.' He donned the jacket and as soon as he zipped up the front, Zainab hooked her arm inside his and they started silently on the ten-minute journey towards the gurdwara.

They reached the gurdwara pretty much at the same time as the procession. Large crowds were assembled outside and Sukhjeet explained that this would be for a prayer to mark the end of the nagar kirtan event, after which Guru Granth Sahib would be respectfully carried out of the float and back to its home inside the gurdwara itself.

Eventually, the crowds started shuffling through the tall, metal car-park gates and into the gurdwara complex itself. As they got close to the gate, Zainab stopped. 'I will see you back at home, Sukhi.' She paused before adding, 'take your time,' grasping his hand and giving it a little farewell rub, whilst smiling warmly.

'You can come in if you want.' Sukhjeet said quietly. 'See what it's like inside? A gurdwara is open to everyone, from any religion.'

'I have my faith Sukhi. But you need yours. Go on, go!'

'You didn't have to come all this way just to see me in, you know.'

'Yes, I did Sukhi. I stood in the window at home watching you thinking about going for ten minutes. But, you didn't. It's OK. Sometimes, we all need a little nudge from our loved ones to do the right thing.'

At that moment, it took all his willpower to overcome an overpowering desire to hug her. However, acutely conscious of his surroundings and the inappropriateness of too much physical contact, he opted for squeezing her hand tightly instead. Starting his shuffle slowly inside with the crowds, he shed a few tears, relieved that he at least managed to turn away from Zainab before he did so, even though they were tears of joy.

There was a long, slow-moving queue to enter the building, deposit your shoes in the cloakroom, climb the stairs and then walk all the way up the long aisle to bow in front of Guru Granth Sahib. Both sides of the main hall were jammed full, men on the right and women on the left. Despite the chill outside, all the fans in the room were whizzing around at high speed to control the stifling heat generated by tightly crammed bodies inside. The logjam didn't bother Sukhjeet. He undid his jacket and queued peacefully, in a reflective trance. The melodious tunes being played and hymns being sung from the main stage, by the same musicians who were in the float earlier, offered a welcome soothing of his soul, like rain falling onto a parched desert. The familiar melodies churned up all sorts of memories from his childhood, his teenage years and the more recent traumatic period. He reflected on just how much his life had transformed from the last few times he had stood in a gurdwara. For sure, he was no longer the happy-go-lucky, naive Sukhi he was with Anita in the Darbar Sahib. But he was also not the despondent Sukhi who had visited the local gurdwara in the village with his parents, the day he left Punjab.

His turn finally came after over an hour. He knelt and bowed his head, opening his soul and subjugating himself entirely to his Creator, as his forehead touched the carpet. *'Vaheguru; I have committed many many wrongs. But most of all, I doubted You and Your plan for me. Forgive me. I pray for the wellbeing of my parents and Zainab....and for all humanity. Guide me in the next steps of my journey on this planet, Vaheguru, Vaheguru, Vaheguru.'* As he arose, he felt a warm glow, deep inside. He had found his way again. Empowered in the knowledge that God was with him in his endeavour, he vowed to go home and tell Zainab just how much she meant to him, tell his parents proudly about her, and work out a way to legitimise his residency in the UK. And for the first time, he found that alongside his determination, he now also possessed absolute confidence that he would succeed.

THE END

ABOUT THE AUTHOR

Jazz was born in inner-city Wolverhampton in 1979, to working class, Punjabi immigrant parents. He studied at Wolverhampton Grammar School, thanks to the 'Assisted Places' social mobility initiative, and subsequently went on to graduate from Cambridge University with a First class master's degree in Engineering. After ten years military service as a pilot in the Royal Air Force, he switched to civil aviation and now flies A380 aircraft for a national airline in the Middle East.

Jazz is married to Amandeep, an international journalist-